MW01257466

King Liz

Fernanda Coppel

A SAMUEL FRENCH ACTING EDITION

SAMUEL FRENCH

FOUNDED 1830

SAMUELFRENCH.COM
SAMUELFRENCH-LONDON.CO.UK

FOR PRODUCTION ENQUIRIES

UNITED STATES AND CANADA
Info@SamuelFrench.com
1-866-598-8449

UNITED KINGDOM AND EUROPE
Plays@SamuelFrench-London.co.uk
020-7255-4302

Each title is subject to availability from Samuel French, depending upon
country of performance. Please be aware that KING LIZ may not be
licensed by Samuel French in your territory. Professional and amateur
producers should contact the nearest Samuel French office or licensing
partner to verify availability.

MUSIC USE NOTE

Licensees are solely responsible for obtaining formal written permission from copyright owners to use copyrighted music in the performance of this play and are strongly cautioned to do so. If no such permission is obtained by the licensee, then the licensee must use only original music that the licensee owns and controls. Licensees are solely responsible and liable for all music clearances and shall indemnify the copyright owners of the play(s) and their licensing agent, Samuel French, against any costs, expenses, losses and liabilities arising from the use of music by licensees. Please contact the appropriate music licensing authority in your territory for the rights to any incidental music.

IMPORTANT BILLING AND CREDIT REQUIREMENTS

If you have obtained performance rights to this title, please refer to your licensing agreement for important billing and credit requirements.

KING LIZ was first produced by Second Stage Theatre in New York City at the McGinn/Cazale Theatre on July 27, 2015. The performance was directed by Lisa Peterson, with sets by Dane Laffrey, costumes by Jessica Pabst, lights by Tyler Micoleau, sound by Darron L. West, and fight direction by Corey Pierno. The Production Stage Manager was Lori Ann Zepp and the Stage Manager was Alisa Zeljeznjak. The cast was as follows:

LIZ RICO	Karen Pittman
GABBY FUENTES	Irene Sofia Lucio
MR. CANDY	Michael Cullen
FREDDIE LUNA	Jeremie Harris
COACH JONES	Russell G. Jones
BARBARA FLOWERS	Caroline Lagerfelt

CHARACTERS

LIZ RICO – 40s, Black or Latina, a powerful sports agent, scares men.

GABBY FUENTES – 30s, Latina, Liz's assistant, a disgruntled overachiever.

MR. CANDY – 60s, the CEO of a top sports agency, self-starter, liberal when it's convenient.

FREDDIE LUNA – 19 years old, Afro-Latino, star basketball player, naïve, defensive, a diamond in the rough.

COACH JONES – 50s, Black, coach of The New York Knicks, terrified of getting fired.

BARBARA FLOWERS – 50s, a world-renowned journalist with a prime time investigative TV show.

SETTING

New York City

TIME

2015

AUTHOR'S NOTE

Liz Rico's entrance at the top of the play is published differently than how I initially wrote and envisioned it. Originally, Liz lip-synced Notorious B.I.G.'s song, "Juicy" and Gabby assisted her in this morning ritual. Sadly, the rights to this song were not attainable for publication, but I hope that the essence of this moment can still live on in future productions. Liz connects to the classic Hip-Hop song "Juicy" because she, like Notorious B.I.G., is a truly self made person, who came from nothing and is now a success story. She starts her day by rapping the beginning lyrics Notorious B.I.G. wrote about making it despite all the people who told him he couldn't do it, he even dedicates the song to these naysayers. In this published version of King Liz, Liz is dancing confidently, with a bold swagger that she exhibits throughout the play, to a Hip-Hop beat. She should embody this same toughness and scrappy energy while she's moving around her office. She's energizing herself for a new day of business by thinking of all the times people said "no" to her. You could even say that she's doing a victory dance in the face of adversity, in the face of the naysayers. This shouldn't be a long beat of dancing nor should it be dance number by any means. This is a beat of Liz in a private moment at work and the audience's introduction to a bold and fierce woman.

ACT ONE

There's Always A List

(Early morning in a large corner office. The walls are covered with pictures of NBA players in fancy frames. A snazzy couch, a mini-bar, and a mahogany desk. The place looks peaceful until...)

*(**GABBY FUENTES**, thirties, Latina, sprints into the room. She's dressed in business professional attire. She carries high heels in one hand and a large coffee in a paper cup in the other.)*

*(The phone rings, **GABBY** doesn't answer, she runs around the room turning on all the lights and pouring the coffee into a coffee mug on the desk. The phone stops ringing, silence. **GABBY** freezes.)*

GABBY. SHIT!

*(The phone rings again. **GABBY** lets out a sigh of relief, she fiddles with the computer on the desk as she answers the phone.)*

Good morn/ ...Yes, yup, boss. Affirmative. Operation morning pump-up in effect.

*(She hangs up the phone and puts on her high heels. She fixes her hair and applies lip gloss, quickly. **GABBY** pulls an iPad from her purse and clicks something on the computer. She puts on sunglasses. **GABBY** sprints to the door. A Hip-Hop beat plays loudly from the computer.)*

(LIZ RICO, 40s, African-American, dressed in a suit, heels, and a gorgeous/elegant coat, enters. LIZ confidently dances around the office as she removes her coat and sips her coffee.)

(GABBY acts as her DJ/hype man, as she controls the music from her iPad [GABBY uses the DJ app to scratch the record, it sounds like music you would hear at a club]. This is routine for them, a choreographed ritual to get LIZ pumped for another day of business.)

(The music stops abruptly.)

(LIZ sits at her desk. GABBY quickly removes her sunglasses, puts away the iPad and heads to her desk. She hands LIZ a stack of folders and a newspaper. It's business as usual. It's as if their morning pump up routine never happened.)

(LIZ checks her email as she speaks.)

LIZ. What is this? Oh, no. No, cancel this meeting with Sullivan. I don't have time for that.

GABBY. Sullivan wanted some advice about a client. We've rescheduled him five times within the past month.

LIZ. Sullivan was begging me for a promotion now Sullivan's just going to have to put on his big boy pants and figure it the fuck out.

GABBY. Okay. Random House called, they want to know how your book is coming along.

LIZ. Tell them it's fan-fucking-tastic.

GABBY. Got it.

LIZ. And don't forget to mention that if they keep hounding me about it I will call Simon & Schuster up. I will, I'll sell them the fucking rights to my future best-selling fucking book. Got it?

GABBY. Yes, Liz.

LIZ. People get out of my way. I feel like making some fucking money today.

(A beat.)

(Both work quietly at their desks. **GABBY** *hesitates to speak, then finally musters up enough courage.)*

GABBY. Liz?

LIZ. Gabby?

GABBY. Can we, perhaps, talk about my...

> *(***LIZ*** *knows what she's referring to but she plays dumb.)*

Last week you said we'd talk about it. Remember?

LIZ. Next week.

GABBY. My landlord raised my rent and I'm the only person I know with an MBA who's about to be homeless.

LIZ. Pencil it in. Too busy today, hun.

GABBY. I...

LIZ. The sooner you schedule the talk, the sooner we can get to it.

> *(***LIZ*** *goes back to reading her emails.)*

Can you get me floor seats for the Nets playoff game? I want to sit next to Deron William's wife. In fact, sit me in the wife section. It's poaching season.

GABBY. Yes. I'm on it Liz.

> *(***GABBY*** *sits at her desk. Defeated.)*

LIZ. Is my lunch set with Phil Jackson?

GABBY. Yes. 12:30, car's coming at noon.

LIZ. Where's the Buddhist turd taking me this time?

GABBY. Jean Georges, do you want me to come and take notes?

LIZ. Nope. He's going to be begging for some trade intel. He's desperate, it won't be pretty.

GABBY. Okay. Well, do you mind if I take an extra ten minutes for lunch today? I have to run to the post office.

LIZ. Absolutely not. Gabby you're very whiny today. Stop it.

> (**GABBY** *quietly types away at her computer. A beat.*)

LIZ. *(reading her computer screen)* I hate this picture of myself, schedule another round of head shots for next week and a facial before that. Charge it to the company card.

GABBY. Got it, Liz.

LIZ. What about Coach Donovan's OKC contract?

GABBY. I took the liberty of reviewing it myself, it looks pretty good.

> (**LIZ** *looks up at* **GABBY** *for the first time since she's been in the office.*)

LIZ. The liberty…

GABBY. I've been here for five years. I've seen thousands of contracts glide over my desk. I figured it was time.

LIZ. Do you know how long I was Mr. Candy's assistant, Gabby? Seven years. Do you know what that's like?

GABBY. I will know in two years.

LIZ. DO NOT touch the contracts unless your name is Liz Rico. Got it?

GABBY. Yes, Liz.

LIZ. Everyone has to pay their dues. How many times do I have to tell you?

GABBY. Five times a day for the past five years.

LIZ. I'll say it another five million times until you get it through that stubborn head.

GABBY. But why? I feel ready.

LIZ. Because "It's good to be king."

GABBY. King? Why? Can't I just ask/ you…

LIZ. Now, now. You'll know when you're king. Many, many years from now. And don't you dare forget about my facial.

(GABBY's fuming. She sits at her desk and angrily types away at her computer. We hear a computer alert sound. GABBY jumps up.)

GABBY. Five Oh. Five Oh.

(LIZ fixes her hair.)

LIZ. What's his ETA?

GABBY. Less than one minute.

(GABBY scrambles to clean up her desk, she spritzes LIZ with perfume then runs to the door with a note pad, ready for...)

(Enter MR. CANDY, 60s, dressed in an expensive suit, hair slicked back. He enters with purpose, ignores GABBY.)

GABBY. Good morning Mr. Candy. Nice suit, Sir. Did you have a good weekend?

MR. CANDY. Liz? You read the news this morning? There's some good stuff on the web.

LIZ. Maybe I did and maybe I didn't.

MR. CANDY. My top agent doesn't the surf the net?

LIZ. I'm very busy Candy, why don't you give me the Cliff Notes?

MR. CANDY. Well, Bleacher Report and ESPN.com had some exquisite top ten lists. In fact, I popped a woody reading them and I usually require assistance in that department.

LIZ. I'll have Gabby look into it. Mr. Candy, now if you'll please excuse me. Gabby can schedule a lunch for us this week to catch up.

MR. CANDY. Not acceptable. I need to speak with you now.

LIZ. You don't pop in on any of the other agents here.

MR. CANDY. Oh, am I inconveniencing you? I'm here to give you a big tip.

LIZ. It's the playoffs and the draft is just around the corner. I've got a lot on my plate here so...

MR. CANDY. I'll have to keep all this in mind the next time you need a favor.

LIZ. Listen, I've been getting calls all month from CAA. They want me and they want me bad. What are you going to do about it?

MR. CANDY. You don't want to go over there. CAA's like fucking purgatory, the underworld, and you're a star, babe.

LIZ. They're offering me a great package, Candy.

MR. CANDY. You can't leave me, we've got history here. Twenty-five years and counting, that doesn't mean anything to you?

GABBY. Twenty-two years, Sir.

*(**MR. CANDY** and **LIZ** ignore **GABBY**.)*

MR. CANDY. Twenty-five years is a long fucking time, Lizzy. I named my first daughter after you.

LIZ. Her name's Cynthia.

MR. CANDY. Her middle name is Elizabeth.

GABBY. It's Cynthia Jane Candy, Sir.

MR. CANDY. Well, I wish her name was Liz. In fact, I'll make some calls and change her name to Liz if that's what it takes.

LIZ. Ya, sure you will. What's the tip?

MR. CANDY. High school guard out of Brooklyn. Athletic freak. He's got a jump shot as pure as the Holy Grail. He's got the flashy passing of Chris Paul and is as quick as Derrick Rose off the dribble. A dynamic dunker. Ball handling capabilities of old school Isaiah Thomas. AND THEN, on top of all that, he's got a nice little step-back three that's un-guardable. We gotta sign him. We gotta sign him now.

LIZ. High school kid? Please. I've got better things to do.

MR. CANDY. Well, that's the thing, he goes to a shitty school down in Red Hook. He's been held back a bunch. He's a nineteen-year-old high school senior. Just barely graduated.

GABBY. Technically he's eligible, he should have graduated last year. We can fudge the details and make it look like he's been out of high school for a year.

MR. CANDY. I saved you the good stuff. He's half Hispanic too, they're hot right now in the press. Mom's illegal or something, had to go back to South America. Kid's been in and out of foster homes and group homes.

LIZ. Quite a sob story Candy. I'm sure this one's gonna be a lot of work.

MR. CANDY. You know how to play the game.

LIZ. Why don't you sign him?

MR. CANDY. I'm not taking on any more clients.

LIZ. Since when?

MR. CANDY. A couple of months. Mrs. Candy won't allow it.

LIZ. Since when do you listen to your wife?

MR. CANDY. There comes a time in every man's life when you're not as quick as you used to be. Your balls droop to your ankles and the R word starts to come into your periphery.

LIZ. R word?

MR. CANDY. Don't make me say it out loud, Liz. In fact, let's just call it an extended leave-of-absence in Florida.

LIZ. I see. Is this a new revelation?

MR. CANDY. I was in with Phil Stern this morning. He seemed to know before the official announcement.

(*LIZ looks to* GABBY. GABBY *types away at her desk and avoids eye contact.*)

LIZ. (*pissed*) Oh he did, did he? Good old Phil Stern knew about this.

MR. CANDY. Don't you worry about him. I'd rather leave the company to you.

LIZ. Can I get that in writing? Gabby, a pen and paper please.

MR. CANDY. Well, it's not that easy. The board has to come to an agreement about who will take over and Phil's at the top of their list. You're both the best agents we've got.

LIZ. I started at this agency when it was just you and me working out of your garage. I've helped build these walls, not Phil Stern.

MR. CANDY. Look, the board is aware of your commitment to this company. Trust me.

LIZ. That's not good enough for me.

MR. CANDY. You're a partner and you run the whole NBA division of the top sports agency in the country. That isn't enough?

LIZ. What's the real reason behind the board's hesitance?

MR. CANDY. There is the intimidation factor. It's not the first time I've had to talk to you about your people skills.

LIZ. Are you kidding me?

MR. CANDY. If you just smiled more. Made more of an effort to be cordial to people, I think it would make a difference.

LIZ. This company is ninety-five percent men and men are scared of me. How is that my problem?

MR. CANDY. Phil Stern keeps great relationships with all the board members.

LIZ. If by "good relationships" you mean Titty Tuesdays down at Penthouse Executive Club, then I can't compete with that.

MR. CANDY. Maybe you will put the board members at ease if…

LIZ. If…

MR. CANDY. Well, this Red Hook kid is going to be a big, big star.

LIZ. How do you know that?

MR. CANDY. You could use a home run, Liz. Something that reminds the board of why you are an asset to the agency and why you deserve to be CEO. This kid's coming at the right time.

LIZ. My twenty-two year career at The Candy Agency is a home run.

MR. CANDY. Imagine, this kid goes early in the draft, gets a Nike deal, a Gatorade commercial, and wins a couple games, yadda, yadda. You make this talented kid a star within the next year and Phil Stern will be reporting to you by next season's draft.

> *(A beat.* **LIZ** *thinks on it.)*

LIZ. What's this kid's name?

> **(GABBY** *keeps typing at her computer and doesn't look up, just responds.)*

GABBY. Federico Luna. Goes by Freddie. Venezuelan Mother, African-American father who died of a gunshot wound to the head by a gang member when Freddie was four. He's the oldest of five. All foster kids that barely see each other because they were placed with different families all over the country.

MR. CANDY. Sign him.

LIZ. I've got a full plate, Candy.

GABBY. I can schedule something for this week. I've already got his address, phone number, and Facebook profile pulled up on my computer.

> *(They ignore* **GABBY**.*)*

LIZ. Why me Candy? Besides impressing the board, why me in particular?

MR. CANDY. You have a similar background.

LIZ. You want me to represent him because we are both from the projects?

MR. CANDY. Maybe you can connect with the kid on that level. And, he's been in trouble with the law.

LIZ. He has a record? How bad are we talking?

GABBY. I've got it right here.

MR. CANDY. Before you look at his files just remember, he's a young man with a lot of potential. And we can't lose him to Jeff Schwartz or Leon Rose for Christ's sake.

LIZ. What were the charges?

GABBY. Assault, battery. Spent some time in Juvie.

(**GABBY** *hands* **LIZ** *a file.*)

MR. CANDY. Sign this kid and work your magic, Liz.

LIZ. This is a tough one, Candy.

MR. CANDY. Oh, come on. You're Liz-fucking-Rico. Where's the song and dance? You're my best fucking showman. Or would you prefer I ask Phil Stern to get this job done?

LIZ. Stern? Stern's from Maine. His idea of the projects is anything below 14th street.

MR. CANDY. I'm keeping the board members hot on you Liz, don't let me down kiddo.

(**MR. CANDY** *exits.*)

(**LIZ** *sits at her desk and goes over the file. She takes out two pictures, they're graphic.*)

GABBY. These are the victims.

LIZ. That kid lost his eye?

GABBY. Yup and he paralyzed that other boy. Allegedly.

(*a beat*)

(**LIZ** *takes a deep breath and exhales.*)

(**GABBY** *brings her another file.*)

GABBY. Here are his high school stats.

(**LIZ** *opens it and reads.*)

LIZ. Fuck.

GABBY. I know.

LIZ. Fuckety freaking fuck.

GABBY. It gets even better.

LIZ. Fucking fucker.

GABBY. The second coming.

LIZ. These can't be right. These are Lebron James' stats, right?

GABBY. Nope, it's Freddie Luna.

LIZ. Are you POSITIVE that these are correct?

GABBY. I triple-checked them with the scouts and the school just now. They are 100 percent accurate.

LIZ. Cancel everything I have today. We're going hunting.

(Lights out.)

Lunch

(A diner.)

*(**LIZ** sits in a booth going over notes.)*

*(**GABBY** enters with hand sanitizer and a rag, she squirts the sanitizer all over the table top and cleans.)*

LIZ. Let's hear it.

GABBY. What?

LIZ. I know you.

GABBY. Know me?

LIZ. You're cleaning the table with contempt. Every wipe is a "Fuck you Liz, I could do this ten times better."

GABBY. That's not it at all. I just wouldn't have brought a potential client here.

LIZ. Oh really? Where would you have scheduled the meeting?

GABBY. The Four Seasons. The office. I could think of ten better places.

LIZ. We are meeting him here because we want to come off as down-to-earth. Trust me. This kid will respond to that more than the Four Seasons.

GABBY. Whatever you say.

LIZ. You want my job. I know it. That's why I hired you.

GABBY. *(scrubs harder)* I'm a tad over qualified for this position but I wanted to learn from the best. So. I'm still here.

LIZ. I sleep with one eye open. You have keys to my penthouse and one of these nights, I just know you're going to sneak in and stab me to death with a letter opener.

GABBY. I'm not sure how to respond to that. I'll be waiting outside for you.

(**LIZ** *opens her mouth as* **GABBY** *sprays some Binaca in it.*)

GABBY. Good luck.

(**GABBY** *begins to exit.*)

LIZ. …Wait.

GABBY. Yes?

LIZ. I'll let you sit at the table with us.

GABBY. REALLY?

LIZ. If you promise to not speak.

GABBY. You won't hear a peep. I swear to God.

LIZ. In fact, I need you to stop breathing. I basically need you to do your best impersonation of a cadaver. Can you do that?

GABBY. *(giddy)* Cadaver. Dead. Got it, Liz.

(**GABBY** *sits next to* **LIZ** *and watches her excitedly.*)

LIZ. Don't do that.

GABBY. Sorry.

(**GABBY** *looks out the window and hums to herself. She excitedly taps her fingers on the table.*)

LIZ. Do you need Ritalin or something?

GABBY. My first time.

LIZ. You've got to treat every deal as if it were your last. You never know when someone's going to pull the rug from under you.

GABBY. You've got this, Liz.

(**LIZ** *doesn't know how to take a compliment. She gives* **GABBY** *a half smile and continues to pour over the files.*)

(*Enter* **FREDDIE LUNA**, *nineteen, handsome and athletic.*)

LIZ. Mr. Freddie Luna?

FREDDIE. 'Sup.

(LIZ and GABBY stand to great him. LIZ extends her hand, FREDDIE doesn't shake it. He gives her a high five.)

LIZ. It's a pleasure to meet you Freddie.

FREDDIE. They got cheeseburgers at this place? The lady on the phone said we'd have cheeseburgers and that you'd be paying.

GABBY. The cheeseburgers are the best in the city, get a double on us. With bacon.

LIZ. This is my assistant Gabby. She's not allowed to speak. Have a seat, please.

(They sit. GABBY fights for positioning in the booth, LIZ shoves her to the side and gives her a dirty look.)

LIZ. You're a little shrimpier than in the pictures.

FREDDIE. You're a little older-looking than your pictures.

LIZ. So you've heard of me.

FREDDIE. Ya. Of course.

LIZ. Good things I hope.

FREDDIE. Jeff Schwartz says that you'll eat the testicles off a new born.

LIZ. Jeff has a very, very small penis.

FREDDIE. Word?

LIZ. Really, it looks like an elevator button. Don't ask how I know that.

FREDDIE. He also said you're a good agent.

GABBY. Uhm, she's the best.

(LIZ stares GABBY down again. GABBY mouths "Sorry.")

FREDDIE. I'm the best player to come outta Red Hook since Carmelo. So, what's your pitch?

LIZ. Pitch?

FREDDIE. I've been on a couple of these so far, lady. You're not impressing me.

LIZ. Oh?

FREDDIE. People are saying that I'll go in the top ten in the draft. People are saying that I've got major endorsements coming my way. I'm kind of a big deal.

LIZ. And so humble.

FREDDIE. Humility doesn't make the Benjamins, you feel me?

LIZ. You're very ambitious. You ready to put in the work?

FREDDIE. I won the state championship, two years in a row. I'm rated number one in the country. That sound like I'm fucking lazy?

LIZ. It sounds like you're talented, but that only gets you so far. A lot of promising players make it to the NBA and drop off the face of the earth. They aren't interested in listening to their coach, putting in the work, or winning. They just wanna get paid, you feel me? Ever heard of Lenny Cooke?

FREDDIE. Lenny who?

LIZ. Exactly. That could be you in five years, boy.

FREDDIE. I doubt it.

LIZ. This business is a graveyard of talented promising players. It can happen to anyone, even you Freddie.

FREDDIE. Why did you ask me here? What can you do for me?

LIZ. This is the reality of your situation. Can you deal? That's the industry you're stepping into. Can. You. Deal.

FREDDIE. The other agents didn't say this shit.

LIZ. I'm not like other agents. I'm really fucking good at my job, look at my client roster. Kevin Love, Carmelo Anthony, Russell Westbrook, Anthony Davis, James Harden. I take talented young guys and I make them international superstars, that's my legacy.

FREDDIE. Jeff Schwartz said I could be the next Jordan.

LIZ. Jeff Schwartz says that to every motherfucker he meets. His client list is also chock full of old geezers.

Paul Pierce, Ray Allen, Kobe Bryant, they are all on their way out.

FREDDIE. All right, I'm gonna be real with you, I've got some obligations.

LIZ. You have kids? Gabby?

(**GABBY** *shrugs nervously and checks her notes.*)

FREDDIE. No, I've got two sisters and two brothers, all younger. We've been in foster care but I want to make enough money so that we can all live together. My mom's in Venezuela struggling to make ends meet. I need to buy her a nice house.

LIZ. That's a lot to put on a boy's shoulders.

FREDDIE. I'm a man. Who the fuck do you think you are?

LIZ. You're a boy but the day you put on that NBA jersey, they'll judge you like a man. The day you sign your first NBA contract you'll kiss your youth goodbye. Are you ready for that?

FREDDIE. Yup.

LIZ. Do you party? Do you do drugs?

FREDDIE. Why the fuck do you care?

LIZ. I'm making an investment. I need to know. Do you do drugs?

FREDDIE. I don't have to answer that.

LIZ. Two words. Len Bias.

FREDDIE. Those aren't two words, that's a name.

LIZ. You know the story?

FREDDIE. Am I even getting my fucking cheeseburger? Or was that a lie?

LIZ. Gifted athlete from Maryland who was drafted to the Celtics in the first round, second pick overall in 1986, died two days later of a drug overdose.

FREDDIE. Ya, so?

LIZ. He really could have been the next Michael Jordan, he was that good. The potential was limitless. Now he's just another statistic. Another stereotype.

FREDDIE. That won't happen to me.

LIZ. You don't just stand for Freddie Luna. You carry a whole community on your shoulders. The press is going to be merciless. The second you fuck up, it fucks it up for all of us. Is your back strong enough to hoist us up? You tell me.

FREDDIE. This is bullshit. You're bullshit.

LIZ. I'm being 100 percent real right now. The honest truth.

FREDDIE. What can you do for me? The other agents offered me cash up front to sign with them. One even showed up with a twenty million dollar Adidas contract, ready for me to sign. What about you?

GABBY. That's completely unethical.

LIZ. I'm not going to offer you a cent, Freddie.

FREDDIE. What's in it for me?

LIZ. The truth. Straight up. I won't sugarcoat it. Trust me, the truth is something that's extinct in this business. In this world.

FREDDIE. The truth, that's it…this meeting is a complete waste of time. Seriously. Who the fuck do you think you are?

LIZ. Let me tell you a little something about who I am.

FREDDIE. I don't want to hear any more of your crap/…

LIZ. My mom died of cancer when I was three because my father couldn't afford her treatment, so when I got a full scholarship to Yale my goal was to grow up to be someone who could pay to kill cancer.

Now I've got a penthouse on the Upper West Side overlooking Central Park, my neighbors are Steven Spielberg and Oprah Winfrey, and I got a house in the Hamptons next door to Commissioner Adam Silver. Within the last three years, my current client roster has collectively made over nine hundred million dollars. I've been the only woman on the Forbes Most Powerful Sports Agents list three times and I've been on Time

Magazine's Most Influential People list twice. Nobody can stop me. No one. Not even God.

GABBY. Oh my God, I have /goosebumps…

LIZ. What I can offer you as an agent isn't anything you can buy. It's my marrow, it's the tenacity that led me to this table. I will fight for you to be successful the way I fought for myself to make it in this world that doesn't want people like us to succeed. I make that promise to you in exchange for a commitment. I need you to promise that you will stay out of trouble.

FREDDIE. You saw my files.

LIZ. Hey, shit happens, right?

FREDDIE. I didn't do it. I was on the wrong street at the wrong time.

LIZ. That happens when you're hanging with the wrong crowd.

FREDDIE. Don't talk to me like that.

LIZ. Like what?

FREDDIE. Like I don't know shit. I know shit, or else we wouldn't be here meeting.

LIZ. Point taken.

FREDDIE. Is my past going to be a problem? Is it going to come up again?

LIZ. You can't allow your past to define you. That's the bottom line. My job is to ensure that your past informs where you want to go. Straight to the top. I want you to be one of those success stories. From Red Hook to the Upper West Side. Shit, I grew up in the projects, too and now look at me.

FREDDIE. Nah, really?

LIZ. I grew up on mayonnaise sandwiches and sugar water, but I worked my ass off to get out. And look at me now. Baby, I run shit.

FREDDIE. I've worked hard too. I wake up at 4 a.m. every morning so I can do conditioning before school. Then after practice I stay on the court 'til 8 p.m. to shoot around with my coach. Then I play pick up games around the neighborhood until 11 p.m. That's my schedule six days a week.

LIZ. That's the kind of dedication I'm talking about. I'm here to help you with the business side of things. Freddie, I've been an agent for a very long time and if there's one thing I've learned it's that white people don't want us, they want our money.

FREDDIE. Meaning?

LIZ. Corporations don't want to hire people like us, they usually have to by law. But they want our money. They need our money so they can continue running the world.

FREDDIE. How are you gonna help keep me in business? When I leave Red Hook, I'm not trying to go back.

LIZ. That's my specialty. I will keep you relevant. We'll create a public persona for you and keep re-creating that persona throughout your career. I've got you. Buy your one way ticket out of this place and join me in Manhattan.

> *(A beat.)*

> *(**FREDDIE**'s starting to be persuaded.)*

FREDDIE. You think I'll go in the top ten?

LIZ. I will ensure that for you, Freddie. I've already called the Knicks and they've expressed a lot of interest.

FREDDIE. They did?

LIZ. I deal with the Knicks all the time. They're good people. I can get you there.

FREDDIE. Empty promises.

LIZ. Not empty. Have you ever Googled me?

FREDDIE. You are a very cocky chick.

LIZ. Call me a chick again and I'll let you sign with Jeff Schwartz and make the biggest mistake of your life.

> *(A beat.)*

> *(**FREDDIE** laughs it off. This lady is the real deal.)*

FREDDIE. You really gonna get me on the Knicks in the first round?

LIZ. Try me. Are you going to listen and keep putting in the work?

> *(**LIZ** extends her hand to **FREDDIE**.)*

FREDDIE. Try me.

> *(They shake on it.)*

GABBY. Waiter? Cheeseburgers, we need a couple cheeseburgers over here STAT.

> *(Lights out.)*

The Draft, Baby

*(The office: it's messier than before. **LIZ** and **GABBY** sit by the TV, the NBA draft is on. They look exhausted and have paperwork surrounding them.)*

*(**GABBY** works on a laptop and wears a phone headset.)*

*(**LIZ** wears a Bluetooth and sips on a Red Bull.)*

(They are both on their respective phone calls.)

LIZ.
You're playing me, Marc. Why the fuck… Cold feet? This kid is the second coming. I'm telling you. His field goal percentage. His defense. He can even shoot the three. He's unique. Fuck you, Marc. Just fuck you *(LIZ hangs up on Marc)* …who do you have? Who do you have? WHO DO YOU HAVE?

GABBY.
Mr. Billy King, Liz is on the other line but she'd really like to speak with you. Can you hold? Please hold. I know it's a busy day but I assure you that it's worth your while to hold. Who is she on the phone with? I shouldn't/ say… Take a wild guess. That's a great guess.

*(**LIZ** snaps wildly at **GABBY**. She's off her call but **GABBY**'s still on the line and wasn't aware that **LIZ** was speaking to her.)*

LIZ. Marc's off. Who do you have??

GABBY. *(covers her receiver)* Are you talking to me?

LIZ. Yes De Niro. Who the fuck do you have on the phone? It's draft day, pay attention.

GABBY. The Nets.

LIZ. Transfer him over. NOW.

GABBY. *(into the phone)* I have Liz Rico, Mr. King.

LIZ. Billy. Big Willy. How are the kids? Oh, good. You know I love you right? Who's my Bill-ster? Who? … You heard about the Mavs? …No, I think Marc is such a dick wad. I… I've been meaning to call you. I want to screw the Mavs. I mean who likes Dallas? Freddie's from Brooklyn. HE WANTS to stay home. I've got your back, Billy. When have I lied to you? When?

(GABBY waves LIZ down.)

GABBY. Knicks. I have the Knicks call coming.

(LIZ does a giddy dance and mimes for GABBY to give her one minute. GABBY answers the call.)

GABBY. Liz Rico's office. Yes, Mr. Mills. Please hold.

LIZ. Billy. I gotta call you back. But don't let me down. Remember our good times at the Draft in '99. No, I wasn't that drunk, Billy. I remember every word. Yes, babe. Okay. You stay strong over there. We wanna go with you. Talk soon. Bye.

(LIZ hangs up the call and takes the next call.)

Steve. Steve-o. My Stevie Wonderful. You know Freddie WANTS to stay local. He's a Brooklyn kid who grew up watching Patrick Ewing and John Starks. He wants to be a Knick. He has a poster of Melo in his locker… Nope. Fuck the Mavs. No, we wanna do business with YOU. Just YOU.

(LIZ high fives GABBY. GABBY turns up the TV. The Commissioner of the NBA speaks.)

COMMISSIONER. The Los Angeles Lakers have selected Anthony Miller from UCLA as their first round pick.

LIZ. You need a superstar guard, Steve. You also need a miracle. I know. I hear you…Well, look at your TV screen because Miller's a Laker now. Yup. I know…

(We hear the crowd go wild on the TV.)

GABBY. *(to LIZ)* Knicks are next.

LIZ. Would I lie to you? Would I? …okay, so I've lied to you but this kid is different… I realize that, but he's matured since then... I assure you. He's a harmless kid, Steve. I'd bet my life on it.

(GABBY's phone rings.)

GABBY. *(to LIZ)* I have Billy on the line.

(LIZ mimes to GABBY that she needs to stall Billy. LIZ mouths "Five minutes.")

LIZ	**GABBY.**
Steve, this would be the biggest mistake of your life. I mean, how will you be able to look your kids in the eye after this? Freddie Luna will be the next Kobe Bryant, the next Chris Paul. I'll let you go then. It's up to you. But I've got the Nets on the other line, Steve. They want him bad, so it's up to you. When Luna scores the game-winning dunk and the Nets sweep you this season, I won't be saying I told you so, I'll just be sipping Cristal and cashing the checks. Buh-Bye.	Good evening, Mr. King. You sound a little sick, do you have a cold? ...Liz will be with you in five short minutes. How's your wife doing? ...I'm not at liberty to tell you who Liz is speaking with... I'm aware of that... Liz is not playing the field, Sir. She's very honest about her client's intention to sign with the Nets. I assure you...

(GABBY waves to LIZ, mimes that LIZ needs to take this call now.)

(LIZ waves for GABBY to transfer the call.)

LIZ. Billy. I missed you... Whoa, whoa. What's with the tone? No I was not on the other line with Steve. I'm committed to you. Freddie Luna wants to be a Net... Are you gonna fuck me over? Your pick is coming up, Billy, put your money where your mouth is.

GABBY. Knicks have one more minute.

(LIZ gives GABBY a thumbs up.)

LIZ. Make the right decision Billy. Listen to your heart.

>*(sings)*

>LISTEN TO YOU HEART.

>Shhhh…just, what does your heart say?

>…okay, okay…how about your gut? Is that telling you anything different? …okay, you should go with your gut here Billy.

GABBY. They are announcing it.

LIZ. I've gotta get going Billy… No it's not because of the Knicks pick… I've gotta go to the bathroom… I have lady needs, all right? Jesus. Talk to you in five. Pick wisely. Bye.

>*(**GABBY** turns up the TV. The NBA **COMMISSIONER** appears again.)*

COMMISSIONER. The New York Knicks have selected Federico Luna from Red Hook High School.

>*(The crowd on the television goes wild.)*

>*(**GABBY** and **LIZ** let out a sigh of relief. They are too exhausted to be excited. **LIZ** takes out her Bluetooth and kicks off her heels. She plops her feet on the couch.)*

GABBY. Martini?

LIZ. Whiskey on the rocks. This one was a real ball buster.

>*(**GABBY**'s phone rings.)*

GABBY. Nets are on the line.

LIZ. Don't answer, that needy bastard needs a shrink NOT me.

GABBY. You played him, Liz.

LIZ. You have to come at all these deals from a place of yes. When the offers come in, then you can be picky. Until then it's "YES. YES. YES."

>*(**GABBY** pours two whiskeys. They clink glasses.)*

GABBY. To Freddie Luna.

LIZ. To US.

> *(They both take sips.* MR. CANDY *enters with a bottle of Champagne. He pops the cork.)*

MR. CANDY. *(Sings)*
FOR SHE'S A JOLLY GOOD FELLOW.
FOR SHE'S A JOLLY GOOD FELLOW.
FOR SHE'S A JOLLY GOOD FELLOW,
WHICH NOBODY CAN DENY.

LIZ. Candy, you have a lovely singing voice.

MR. CANDY. WE DID IT KIDDO!

GABBY. We?

MR. CANDY. Get us a couple glasses, would you? Uh...

LIZ. Gabby.

MR. CANDY. Gabby, yes. The nice crystal glasses in my office.

> *(GABBY exits. Disgruntled.)*

MR. CANDY. You did it again.

LIZ. Are you surprised? I've been doing it for twenty-two years.

MR. CANDY. Can't we sit and enjoy the fruits of our labor for one minute?

LIZ. Okay. All right.

> *(They sit quietly. Not much to say.* MR. CANDY *looks around her office.)*

MR. CANDY. I like what you've done with the place.

LIZ. I've been in this office for ten years.

MR. CANDY. Why don't you have any African art up on the walls? Berry in accounting has this great African art up, he's really proud of it.

LIZ. Just because Berry and I are both Black doesn't mean that we are going to decorate our office the same way.

MR. CANDY. I know. I know. I'm just saying. Be proud of your heritage, it's unique and exotic.

LIZ. Do you have white artists plastered all over your walls?

MR. CANDY. Not specifically, no.

LIZ. You're not proud of your heritage?

MR. CANDY. Don't get defensive. You're always getting so defensive. That's my biggest criticism of you after all these years.

LIZ. Uh huh.

MR. CANDY. Be proud of your heritage. Be proud of your past.

LIZ. That's not the issue.

MR. CANDY. I'm just so proud of you. I've seen you work so hard... Can I confess something to you Liz? Do you mind?

LIZ. Yes but try your hardest not to be offensive.

MR. CANDY. Well, ever since your father passed away, I've felt like your father figure. Like your father passed the reins on to me.

LIZ. But you have your own children that you never see.

MR. CANDY. I've been looking out for you, it's an instinct. And secretly I've been hoping you would find a nice man to marry who could take care of you. So I wouldn't have to worry about you so much.

LIZ. I can take care of myself, did that ever occur to you?

MR. CANDY. I know you can but as a father, you want the best for your daughters. Safety. Good man by her side.

LIZ. You're not my father, Mr. Candy. You're my boss. It's a very different type of relationship.

MR. CANDY. I feel comfortable with you Lizzie. Think of it as a compliment.

LIZ. Lucky me.

MR. CANDY. Listen, the board is going bananas over the Luna kid. They couldn't be happier with the good publicity. My assistant caught Phil Stern masturbating while crying in the men's room. You're in the lead, my dear.

LIZ. Are you surprised?

MR. CANDY. You going to miss me around here?

LIZ. Kind of, I guess.

MR. CANDY. You guess?

LIZ. I'm sure you'll be around.

MR. CANDY. Nope. I'll be out of your hair forever.

LIZ. You'll be calling me every five minutes.

MR. CANDY. No, no. I'm leaving the place in good hands. I'll back off.

> (**GABBY** *returns with two champagne glasses as* **MR. CANDY** *gets up to leave.*)

MR. CANDY. Catch you later, my little supernova.

> (**MR. CANDY** *exits.*)

GABBY. What did I miss?

LIZ. Pour it. One for you, too.

> (**GABBY** *pours the champagne and they toast.*)

LIZ. To all the motherfuckers who want a piece of you when you're on top.

GABBY. Like Mr. Candy?

LIZ. You remember this Gabby. You remember how hard we worked and how fast someone else pranced in here to take all the credit.

> (**LIZ** *downs her champagne.*)

> (**GABBY** *watches her.*)

> (*Lights out.*)

Welcome To The Pros, Now Fuck Off

(An office. **FREDDIE LUNA** *and* **LIZ** *sit.* **FREDDIE** *'s nervous, he keeps fidgeting.)*

*(***LIZ** *checks emails.)*

*(***FREDDIE** *starts to beat box. He starts to dance along to the beat. He gets into it.)*

*(***LIZ** *slaps* **FREDDIE** *upside the head.)*

LIZ. Grow the fuck up.

FREDDIE. I'm grown.

LIZ. Sit up straight. Stop moving around in your chair. You look like a lizard on coke.

FREDDIE. Coach Jones is someone I really look up to, I wanna make a good impression.

LIZ. Tuck in your shirt and don't say anything stupid.

FREDDIE. When I was little my mom would sing to me when I was scared.

LIZ. No fucking way, buddy.

FREDDIE. She would sing in Spanish. It really calms me down.

LIZ. Take a Xanax like a mature person.

FREDDIE. I just wanna do a good job. This is the only way I know how.

*(***LIZ** *makes a call on her cell.)*

LIZ. Get in here.

*(***GABBY** *enters before* **LIZ** *can hang up the phone.)*

GABBY. Did I forget something? I'm so sorry if I forgot something. I swear I triple-checked all the arrangements last night and again this morning.

LIZ. Shut up and sing something.

GABBY. Excuse me?

LIZ. Sing in Spanish, for Freddie.

GABBY. Uh.

LIZ. Name a song Freddie.

GABBY. This is kind of racist, Liz.

FREDDIE. I don't know the names of the songs. I was little.

LIZ. Sing, Gabby. Something traditional.

> (*A beat.* **GABBY** *thinks, but nothing is coming to mind.*)

LIZ. Just do it!

> (**GABBY'S** *still thinking, then it hits her.*)

GABBY. (*sings*)
    DE LA SIERRA MORENA,
    CIELITO LINDO, VIENEN BAJANDO ...

FREDDIE. Oh snap, I know this song. I love this shit.

GABBY. Sing it with me, Liz.

FREDDIE. Yes! Come on, Liz. We're all nervous.

LIZ. I don't speak Spanish.

GABBY. But I got you Rosetta Stone for Christmas?

LIZ. Oops.

FREDDIE. How can you not speak Spanish? Get Leon Rose on the phone. He speaks it fluently.

LIZ. You're killing me kid. Killing me.

> (**GABBY** *and* **FREDDIE** *sing together.* **FREDDIE**'*s smiling and enjoying himself.* **LIZ** *works on her phone.*)

GABBY & FREDDIE.
    UN PAR DE OJITOS NEGROS,
    CIELITO LINDO, DE CONTRABANDO.

GABBY. Why don't you come in on the chorus, Liz?

LIZ. Why don't you look for another job, Gabby?

> (**FREDDIE** *takes out his phone and pretends to dial.*)

FREDDIE. Hello? CAA? Ya, I need to speak with Leon Rose please?

*(**LIZ** groans and puts her phone down. She half-heartedly hums along.)*

GABBY, FREDDIE.
AY, AY, AY, AY,
CANTA Y NO LLORES,
PORQUE CANTANDO SE ALEGRAN,
CIELITO LINDO, LOS CORAZONES.

LIZ. All right. Okay. All right. This isn't therapy, kid. Gabby? Meet you outside.

GABBY. Sure.

*(**GABBY** smiles and exits.)*

FREDDIE. She's the best.

LIZ. I'm the best. She's my assistant.

FREDDIE. Jealous?

LIZ. Did Gabby get you here? Or did I?

FREDDIE. I've been thinking a lot about you Liz.

LIZ. You have?

FREDDIE. Why the fuck would anyone want to be an agent? It's the fucking worst job in the universe.

LIZ. Yep. It's pretty bad.

FREDDIE. I mean you don't really do anything and you take four percent of my money. What the fuck do you even do all day?

LIZ. I do a lot, kid.

FREDDIE. Like what?

LIZ. I ensured this deal. The Knicks deal? Twenty million for three years. I got you a shit load of money.

FREDDIE. Ya but how?

LIZ. Let's put it this way: I do all the things that nobody else wants to do. I lie, cheat, and steal for my clients. I make sure they're rich.

FREDDIE. So you just woke up one day and said to yourself "I want to be an agent."

LIZ. I was a basketball player, played for Yale back in the day.

FREDDIE. What position?

LIZ. Point guard. Had a mean crossover.

FREDDIE. Seriously.

LIZ. To this day I'm convinced that Allen Iverson stole my moves. He was six or seven years old when we won the NCAA championship and it was nationally televised. I know that asswipe stole my game.

FREDDIE. You're fucking nuts Liz. I love it.

> (**COACH JONES**, *fifties, Black, enters. He wears a tracksuit and chews gum profusely.*)

COACH JONES. Liz.

LIZ. Coach, good to be doing business with you.

COACH JONES. Always a pleasure.

> (**COACH JONES** *hugs* **LIZ** *warmly.*)

LIZ. Is that an iPhone 6 in your pocket or are you happy to see me, Coach?

COACH JONES. Maybe a little of both.

LIZ. Allow me to introduce you to this future hall-of-famer. Federico Luna.

> (**FREDDIE** *extends his hand to* **COACH JONES**, *they shake hands.*)

FREDDIE. It's a real honor, sir.

COACH JONES. Call me Coach.

FREDDIE. Coach I... I've read all your books. I think you're one of the greatest coaches of all time. I can't believe you are my coach. I... I'm your best player.

LIZ. He's a little nervous.

COACH JONES. Do you want some water, kid?

FREDDIE. I meant to say, you will make me a better player.

COACH JONES. Right. Good.

LIZ. We are thrilled to be with this franchise, Coach.

COACH JONES. I see that. I feel it. Liz you mind letting us talk man-to-man here? I mean you won't be around the majority of the season. I'd like to get to know Freddie one-on-one.

LIZ. Okay. Sure. I'll be waiting outside if you need me, okay Freddie?

> (**LIZ** *opens the door to leave, we hear her scream for* **GABBY**.*)*

GABBYYYYY? GAAAABY??

> (**LIZ** *exits.*)

> (*A beat.*)

> (**COACH JONES** *stares at* **FREDDIE** *intensely. It's searing.* **FREDDIE** *feels warm/nervous, he grins at him.*)

FREDDIE. Coach Jones, holy shit. I can't believe you're my coach, sir.

COACH JONES. You better. This is all very real, son.

FREDDIE. I didn't mean it like that. I just really look up to you, Coach.

COACH JONES. Uh huh. Okay. You have some great stats, Luna.

FREDDIE. I'm ready to play coach, I'm locked in.

COACH JONES. You averaged a triple double every game last season. Two-time state champ. That's all pretty good… for high school.

> (*A beat.* **FREDDIE** *doesn't know how to respond.*)

There's a big difference between playing against a bunch of teenagers and playing against professional athletes. Do you think you're ready? Or do you just need the money? That happens a lot nowadays.

FREDDIE. I'm ready to play, that's all you need to know.

COACH JONES. Uh huh. Uh huh. What about your criminal record? Those assault charges. That something I need to worry about?

FREDDIE. I was at the wrong place at the wrong time, sir.

COACH JONES. But I heard you have a temper. I heard that it's possible that you actually beat the shit out of those kids.

FREDDIE. I'm telling you the facts. The truth. I'm a lot of things but I'm not a liar.

COACH JONES. Answer the question, do you have a temper? Do I need to worry about technical fouls here?

FREDDIE. I mean, I get passionate, sir. I'm not going to lie.

COACH JONES. Latrell Sprewell passionate? Another Ron Artest?

FREDDIE. I just like to win. That a bad thing coach?

COACH JONES. When do you turn twenty?

FREDDIE. January.

COACH JONES. Capricorn.

FREDDIE. Hm?

COACH JONES. Astrology.

FREDDIE. That matter?

COACH JONES. Just trying to get a sense of you. I don't normally like Capricorns.

FREDDIE. I don't even know what that means, sir.

> *(A beat.)*

> *(**COACH** continues to stare at **FREDDIE**.)*

COACH JONES. I'm going to be honest with you. I didn't want to draft you.

FREDDIE. Oh?

COACH JONES. I wanted us to draft Anthony Miller. He's led UCLA to the Final Four, twice, he's poised, mature AND he has great stats.

FREDDIE. Anthony Miller?

COACH JONES. But fuck me. Last year our record was the laughing stock of the league and I don't have a say within this doomed organization.

FREDDIE. Word? You seem powerful, sir.

COACH JONES. Listen. If Anthony Miller was here we'd have a shot at winning some games this year. But the higher ups just want us to sell tickets and entertain a bunch of beer drinking assholes with hot dogs sticking out of their dick-sucking lips. Instead of a championship contender, they drafted me a fucking baby. I'm not a coach. I'm a babysitter.

FREDDIE. I…uh.

COACH JONES. I'm gonna make this really easy for you, okay?

FREDDIE. Okay, ya.

COACH JONES. Show up. Don't do anything stupid. Don't make me look bad. I like my job, I've been here for a couple of years and the front office has stuck with me. The second we start losing again, the second some baby throws a tantrum on the bench, then my ass is out on the street. So don't fuck up or I will kill you. Got it?

FREDDIE. I got it, sir.

COACH JONES. Glad we had this chat. See you in practice.

> (**COACH JONES** *shakes* **FREDDIE***'s hand. Meeting's over as far as he's concerned.*)

FREDDIE. That's it?

COACH JONES. Oh sorry, did you want me to roll out the fucking red carpet you little shit?

FREDDIE. No sir, I just wanted a little direction. My goal is to start.

COACH JONES. Start?

FREDDIE. I'll work hard. I'll do whatever you say, Coach. I just want to start.

COACH JONES. So I start you, then what?

FREDDIE. I'd be eternally grateful.

> (**COACH JONES** *puts his head in his hands, lets out a deep sigh. This kid doesn't get it.*)

COACH JONES. It's not about you, idiot.

FREDDIE. Okay?

COACH JONES. Get out of my office you fucking baby.

FREDDIE. Okay. Uh, thanks Coach.

COACH JONES. Welcome to the pros. Get out.

(**FREDDIE** *exits, his dignity is barely intact.*)

(**COACH JONES** *works at his desk quietly for a beat.*)

(**LIZ** *enters without knocking.*)

LIZ. What did you say to that boy?

COACH JONES. Mom's back.

(**LIZ** *shuts* **COACH JONES**' *door and rolls up her sleeves.*)

LIZ. You're sitting on a winning lottery ticket. You're not going to cash it in because you wanted Anthony fucking Miller?

COACH JONES. That kid is not a winning lottery ticket, he's a publicity stunt.

LIZ. He has natural talent, sure, it's raw but you're a coach. You're supposed to help him grow. He could be the biggest success story of your sad-ass career Jones.

COACH JONES. I feel like we are looking at one of those 3D posters. You see a whole landscape there, a utopia. I see a wasteland, honey. Just the way it goes.

LIZ. Do not bench him, Jones. I repeat, do not bench this kid.

COACH JONES. I will until he shows me something in practice.

LIZ. You sorry sack of shit.

COACH JONES. I love it when you talk dirty.

LIZ. Your ego's getting in the way.

COACH JONES. It's not my ego. It's child support, it's alimony. I can't afford to lose my fucking job right now. I just can't.

LIZ. You need to give this kid a chance.

COACH JONES. Why? Cuz you want the endorsements? Cuz you want the publicity? I worked my ass off to get this position. I assisted ten teams, paid my fucking dues. Now this kid is gonna have to do the same. Shit, even Kobe Bryant came off the bench his rookie year.

LIZ. Coach Jones, you have the opportunity to mold your own Kobe or Kevin Garnett or Lebron James.

COACH JONES. So what you're saying is that I should just roll up my sleeves, put in the work so you can cash the checks.

LIZ. I'm saying it will benefit you.

COACH JONES. You and I both know that if anything goes wrong the coach is the first to go.

LIZ. Do you want to be an average employed coach? Or do you want to be a heroic hall-of-famer?

COACH JONES. What the fuck do you think Liz?

LIZ. Good coaches have good records and then they fall off the face of the earth. Great coaches make an impact, they touch people. They put themselves on the line. Did your ex-wife chop your balls off? Or were you born a eunuch?

COACH JONES. You've been pushing me around for years, but this time it's not gonna work. I'm absolutely right about that kid. You won't pressure me into thinking differently.

LIZ. I'm crying for you. On the inside, I'm a river of tears. Poor you. Your boss drafted you a young athletic guard with promise. I mean, this kid is nineteen, he's got zero miles on the speedometer. You're looking at fourteen years in this league. That's so many championships. That's so many MVP awards. That's so many "Coach of the Year" awards.

COACH JONES. …I'll see.

LIZ. Sure. Sure.

COACH JONES. He's gotta do well in training camp.

LIZ. Of course.

COACH JONES. And he's gotta listen to every word I say.

LIZ. I love it when you assert whatever shred of ego you have even after you've realized that I'm completely right. It's cute.

    (**LIZ** *exits*. **COACH JONES** *throws a pen at the door.*)

COACH JONES. Fucking bitch!!

    (Lights out.)

This Fool

*(**LIZ**'s office, weeks later.)*

*(**LIZ** has her shoes off and dribbles a basketball nervously. She skillfully bounces the ball between her legs.)*

*(**GABBY** enters quickly, she's on her cell phone.)*

LIZ. Is he here? Is he??

*(**GABBY** waves her off, she's trying to hear the person on the phone.)*

LIZ. Is that him? I will end him if he doesn't get up here.

GABBY. He brought an entourage, they are causing a raucous at security.

LIZ. That insignificant spec of feces.

GABBY. I'll get him up here alone. Take a deep breath.

*(**GABBY** exits. **LIZ** continues dribbling.)*

LIZ. Deep breath… I love my job. I love my job. My clients are immature prepubescent morons BUT I love my job. I love my job.

*(**GABBY** re-enters with **FREDDIE**, he's cussing **GABBY** out. He's fuming.)*

FREDDIE. THIS IS BULLSHIT. MOTHERFUCKING BULLSHIT.

GABBY. Shhh, this is a place of business.

FREDDIE. My boys are down there getting harassed by security. You hear me? Huh? You hear me you dumb bitch??

*(A fearful **GABBY** walks to her desk. **LIZ** approaches a heated **FREDDIE**, she gets in his face. She's not scared of him.)*

LIZ. You're the dumbest bitch around here as far as I'm concerned.

FREDDIE. Fuck you, don't call me a bitch.

LIZ. Sit down boy. And SHUT UP.

FREDDIE. I'll stand.

> (LIZ *grabs* FREDDIE *by the ear and forces him to sit on her couch.*)

LIZ. Sit your ass down.

FREDDIE. Ouch. Ouch.

LIZ. Where were you today? Peter Roth from Puma waited for an hour and a half for you.

FREDDIE. Puma sucks, I prefer Nike.

LIZ. Oh, so Puma isn't your preference. That's it. Did you get that Gabby?

> (GABBY *nods and rolls her eyes.*)

LIZ. So the seventy million dollars you cost me today, was that also not your preference?

FREDDIE. Oops.

LIZ. This is fucking business, Freddie. Don't fuck with me and my legacy.

FREDDIE. I got held up with my boys.

LIZ. Peter from Puma flew in from Germany to meet with you.

FREDDIE. Fine, I'll meet with him.

GABBY. Peter didn't want to reschedule, the meeting's cancelled for good.

FREDDIE. Shut up, bitch. No one's talking to you until you let my boys upstairs.

LIZ. You call her or any female a bitch in my presence again and I will whoop your ass all the way back to the projects. Got it?

FREDDIE. Ya.

LIZ. Ya, what?

FREDDIE. Yes, Ma'am.

LIZ. Now, what the fuck is really going on.

FREDDIE. Nothing.

LIZ. I could have a seventy million dollar contract on my desk right now, but I don't. I need an explanation.

FREDDIE. I was hanging with my boys, we went shopping on 34th street.

LIZ. Who was paying?

FREDDIE. Look, I'm sorry I missed the meeting.

LIZ. Do your boys know what you did today?

FREDDIE. They don't care.

LIZ. Do you care?

FREDDIE. I guess.

LIZ. If you don't care, then what the fuck am I doing here? I'm putting in the work.

FREDDIE. And I'm not?

LIZ. You gotta show up for yourself. At the end of the day when you rest your pretty little head down on your pillow, you have to be able to tell yourself that you tried your best that day. Can you say that about today?

FREDDIE. …guess not.

LIZ. Nope. You did a shitty job. You get an F in life today.

FREDDIE. I'm a great player and I work hard on the court. My boys know it's true.

LIZ. You know what I think?

FREDDIE. I don't give a/ fuck.

LIZ. You're scared shitless and your boys only feed into your insecurities.

FREDDIE. Maybe. Maybe.

LIZ. Quit acting like a moody teenager.

FREDDIE. Things are changing fast Liz, I'm getting recognized on the street all the time. This morning I had my first paparazzi experience.

LIZ. Get used to it, it's part of the business.

FREDDIE. I was walking around Midtown. Usually, I blended in with the packs of tourists and business dudes but today this hot girl stopped me and started shouting,

"You're a Knick! Can we take a selfie?" I was like, "With me? Sure, okay."

Then another guy was like "Yo, Freddie Luna you're gonna lead the Knicks to a championship." Pretty soon a sea of fans crowded around me wanting my autograph. I felt like I was Lebron James strutting around Cleveland, like I was Michael Jordan swagadelically walking around Chicago, like I was Kobe Bryant striding around L.A. I'm THE GUY and this is MY CITY now. It was like a dream until this fat asshole with a camera ran up. He stuck a super bright light in my face and started asking me questions about my case. The crowd started leaving. Some fans started looking at me like I was a criminal. The paparazzi guy just kept naming shit off my rap sheet, asking me what it's like in Juvie. He even asked me if I dropped the soap.

LIZ. What did you say?

FREDDIE. I just kept walking but he was bothering me, "Freddie are you aware that the victims have started a Boycott Freddie Luna Facebook page?"

LIZ. Bullshit, once you start winning everyone will get amnesia. That's the way it goes.

FREDDIE. I told you, I didn't hurt those guys/ I was…

LIZ. Shh. I don't wanna know. I don't need to know.

FREDDIE. You've gotta believe me.

LIZ. It doesn't matter what I think, Freddie.

FREDDIE. It matters to ME. If you want me to trust you, you've gotta believe me.

LIZ. I don't know what I think.

FREDDIE. I wouldn't hurt anyone like that. Swear to God. And I'm no snitch either. I took the fall like a man. Shit, where I come from that's a noble thing to do for a friend.

LIZ. What did your friend do for you?

FREDDIE. He doesn't have to do anything, it's called loyalty.

LIZ. Where's my loyalty? You made me look really bad today, Freddie. Where's my loyalty?

FREDDIE. Say it.

LIZ. Okay, fine. I believe you. All right? Now don't ever tarnish my good name again? GOT IT?

FREDDIE. Say it like you mean it.

LIZ. Don't give me a line reading, boy.

FREDDIE. Seriously. Say it for real.

LIZ. Freddie, I believe that you are an innocent man.

> *(A beat.)*

> *(**FREDDIE** grabs **LIZ'S** hand and squeezes it tightly. He puts her hand over his heart and holds it there for a moment.)*

FREDDIE. Thank you, Liz. Thank you so much.

> *(A beat.)*

> *(**LIZ** is moved by **FREDDIE**'s sincerity; he just wanted someone to believe him.)*

> *(Lights out.)*

Buzzer Beater

*(Weeks later. **LIZ'S** office, late night. **LIZ** and **GABBY** work side by side.)*

(The basketball game is on TV. The Knicks vs. The Heat.)

LIZ. Nike call back?

GABBY. Nope.

LIZ. Gatorade?

GABBY. Nope.

LIZ. Subway?

GABBY. Nope.

LIZ. Trojan condoms?

GABBY. No, no one called. For the millionth time.

(A beat, they work quietly.)

You think Peter Roth from Puma spread the word about Freddie's accountability issue?

LIZ. Don't ask me stupid questions, Gabby. Just put some bourbon in your coffee and keep working.

GABBY. He's a good player and he has star quality.

LIZ. He's playing shitty and he pissed an important person off.

GABBY. He's a rookie.

LIZ. Well, in tonight's game he's gotten dunked on by the whole Heat organization. Pat Riley could suit up and dunk on his ass.

GABBY. What should we do?

LIZ. Just sit and wait. The kid's just nervous. It happens.

*(**GABBY** watches the game for a moment, Dwayne Wade dunks on **FREDDIE**.)*

*(**GABBY** and **LIZ** respond as if they've just witnessed a car crash.)*

GABBY.	LIZ.
Oh shit.	That's gotta hurt.

NBA ANNOUNCER. Wow! That's some vintage Dwyane Wade stuffing it down Luna's throat. Welcome to the NBA kid. And the Heat are up by two with 6.8 seconds left in the Fourth. Knicks have the ball.

GABBY. It's a close game. They could come back. The Knicks will pull through and win this game, right?

LIZ. Off the record?

GABBY. Ya, just between us.

LIZ. Not a chance in hell.

GABBY. So how do we get endorsements?

LIZ. Call the WME talent department. Maybe we can get him a famous girlfriend?

GABBY. Who?

LIZ. Someone cute and young. Someone on TV, like an edgy cable show.

GABBY. I don't have time to watch TV.

LIZ. Google it.

(*LIZ* and **GABBY** *watch the game.*)

NBA ANNOUNCER. Galloway will inbound the ball. Anthony's double-teamed. Hardaway's being hounded by his man. Calderon's fighting to get free, Knicks need to get the ball in fast. Nobody's open, except… the rookie's open? Luna, the rookie's wide open. Luna gets the inbound pass.

(*LIZ* and **GABBY** *jump up.*)

LIZ. HOLY CRAP!

GABBY. Get it Freddie!

LIZ. DON'T FUCK THIS UP.

GABBY. SHOOT! SHOOT!

NBA ANNOUNCER. Luna dribbles out. Bosh and Wade come to help. Luna pump fakes and shoots the three and… IT'S GOOD!! KNICKS BEAT THE HEAT. THE

ROOKIE WINS THE GAME. LUNA WINS THE GAME
in an incredible shot right over Dwayne Wade!!!

LIZ. HOLY SHIT/ HOLY SHIT.

> *(LIZ and GABBY are screaming, they hug each other while jumping up and down.)*
>
> *(The office phone begins to ring.)*
>
> *(LIZ's cell phone begins to ring.)*
>
> *(GABBY's cell phone begins to ring.)*
>
> *(Lights out.)*

Big Shot

(A press conference.)

*(**COACH JONES** is answering a question from a reporter. He's giddy.)*

COACH JONES. …game was a close one. But, we really came out and competed. I mean, The Heat are a talented team and we really gave them a hard time on the defensive end. Bosh struggled, Wade struggled, and now that James went home they have no one to bail them out offensively. *(The press laughs.)* But on a serious note, I'm very proud of our guys. Very proud.

REPORTER. Did you draw up that last play for the rookie, Luna?

COACH JONES. The last play was not drawn up for Freddie. But, he was open and he made the shot.

REPORTER. If he had missed the shot, would there have been consequences?

COACH JONES. I'd rather not answer that.

REPORTER. It's common sense, if a rookie doesn't listen to his coach it's usually off with his head.

COACH JONES. I wanna keep it positive, this win really boosted our confidence. Freddie's an ambitious young player with a lot of talent. He's proved to me tonight that he can handle the pressure.

REPORTER. Do you think Luna will get "Rookie of the Year?"

COACH JONES. I hope so. I'd love that for him.

*(**FREDDIE** enters with **LIZ**. They are glowing.)*

COACH JONES. Liz?

LIZ. *(beaming)* Great game, Coach! Everyone, I present to you future Rookie of the Year Freddie Luna.

*(The press clap for **FREDDIE** as does **COACH JONES**. **FREDDIE** loves the attention.)*

FREDDIE. Thanks Coach, thanks Liz.

COACH JONES. The day we drafted this kid was a great day for this franchise. Have a seat, son. The man of the hour, folks.

(**FREDDIE** *and* **LIZ** *sit.*)

COACH JONES. Freddie's overbearing agent will be joining us.

(**LIZ** *rolls her eyes, the media laugh.*)

FREDDIE. She's the best.

LIZ. That's Liz Rico. R-I-C-O.

REPORTER. Freddie, great shot. How do you feel?

FREDDIE. Yo, I'm just happy it went in.

(*The media and* **COACH JONES** *laugh.*)

LIZ. He's being modest. Talk them through it, Freddie.

FREDDIE. For real though, I wanted the ball. I knew I could do it. And I did.

REPORTER. That's a lot of confidence for someone with a rough start to your rookie season. Averaging 2.2 points a game and one rebound. How were you able to bounce back?

FREDDIE. Don't know, I just got the opportunity tonight to prove myself and I, uh… I look forward to proving myself in the future.

REPORTER. Coach: do you think Luna will be your clutch player from now on? Has he earned that spot?

COACH JONES. He takes the credit tonight and as for the future he just needs to keep up the good work.

REPORTER. Freddie: How did it feel to shoot over a future hall-of-famer and three-time NBA champion Dwyane Wade?

FREDDIE. To be honest, I loved it. I want to be the best, so.

REPORTER. Freddie: there are some reports going around about your past. Do you care to respond to that?

LIZ. No comment.

COACH JONES. We just wanna talk about the game.

FREDDIE. What kind of stuff?

REPORTER. Your criminal record.

FREDDIE. Oh. I mean, that's not something we gotta talk about, right?

LIZ. Right. Next question?

REPORTER. There are reports that two of the victims you assaulted were in the crowd tonight.

>   (COACH JONES *tries to deflect the question.* FREDDIE*'s rage begins to bubble.*)

COACH JONES. A lot of people come to the games, there is no way to confirm that.

REPORTER. We've confirmed their tickets and seats. They've been yelling obscenities at Freddie, hoping he will play poorly.

LIZ. Madison Square Garden is one of the loudest stadiums in the league. He can't hear all the conversations going on. He's focused on the game.

REPORTER. Freddie do you hear them? They have a group that's been yelling and tonight they threw trash at you.

FREDDIE. I didn't do shit, man.

LIZ. Calm down.

REPORTER. So you do hear them?

FREDDIE. Fuck them.

LIZ. Freddie.

FREDDIE. Those motherfuckers wanna waste their money on tickets just to fuck with my head. They can do that, but I didn't hurt those guys.

COACH JONES. *(to* FREDDIE*)* Relax.

REPORTER. You were convicted and served time, right?

FREDDIE. I won the game, doesn't that mean anything to you people?

LIZ. Coach? Let's wrap this up.

COACH JONES. Good idea. That's all for tonight folks, thanks.

>   (COACH JONES *and* LIZ *start to stand, they try to get* FREDDIE *to leave.*)

REPORTER. We confirmed all this with the New York State courts.

> (**FREDDIE** *still seated slams his hand on the table.*)

FREDDIE. Man, I said I didn't want to talk about this.

LIZ. You don't have to.

FREDDIE. I'm fucking past that shit, Liz.

REPORTER. He answered the question.

COACH JONES. Look, this is his first post-game interview. Cut him a break.

REPORTER. Freddie, can you confirm that you assaulted those boys and served time for the crimes you committed?

LIZ. Get your ass up.

> (**COACH JONES** *tries to get* **FREDDIE** *out of his chair.* **FREDDIE** *pushes* **COACH JONES** *off of him.* **COACH JONES** *doesn't budge, he continues helping* **FREDDIE** *out of his chair.*)

FREDDIE. FUCK you. FUCK ALL OF YOU. I'M A KNICK.

COACH JONES. Quiet, let's get going.

LIZ. This press conference is officially OVER.

FREDDIE. I'M A MOTHERFUCKING KNICK NOW, OKAY??

LIZ. Good night everyone.

REPORTER. Freddie! Freddie one more question!!

> (**FREDDIE** *pushes* **COACH JONES** *harder. This time* **COACH JONES** *flies backwards.*)

> (**FREDDIE** *stands to see if* **COACH JONES** *is okay.* **LIZ** *tries to block* **FREDDIE** *from the press, but the cameras start to flash wildly.*)

FREDDIE. LOOK WHAT YOU MADE ME DO. I shouldn't have to deal with this shit anymore. YOU HEAR ME?

> (*Lights out.*)

End of Act One

ACT TWO

Grounded

(A nice hotel room. We hear the shower running. It turns off.)

*(**FREDDIE LUNA** emerges from a steamy bathroom. He's got a towel wrapped around his waist.)*

(He stands in front of a mirror looking at himself.)

(A beat. He has no idea who he is. He takes a deep breath and lets it out.)

FREDDIE. *(to himself)* Come on now. Man up. You got this.

*(**FREDDIE** walks over to the bed. He sits for a moment, then turns on the TV. He changes channels, we hear different shows in the background.)*

*(ESPN's Sports Center theme song starts to play. **FREDDIE** watches as we hear the announcers.)*

TV ANNOUNCER. Top story tonight is Freddie Luna. The rookie guard for the Knicks is causing quite a stir around the league. During last night's press conference he pushed his coach to the ground. Bobby, I gotta tell you, some guys they just aren't ready for the NBA. It's not just about skill. It's not just about talent. It's really about maturity. This kid's behaving like a thug with a criminal past. But he's a professional athlete, he needs to grow up…

FREDDIE. Man, you don't know me.

(**FREDDIE** *turns off the TV; he's furious. He paces the room in his towel.*)

(*A beat. He takes a deep breath and tries to calm himself. That doesn't work. He goes to the bed and punches the shit out of some pillows.*)

(*He stops. He feels a little bit better. He goes to the closet and slides open the door.*)

(**LIZ RICO** *pops out.* **FREDDIE** *jumps back.*)

FREDDIE. HOLY /FUCK

LIZ. I know this is weird.

FREDDIE. SHIT. HOLY SHIT/ THIS IS BULLSHIT.

LIZ. Drastic times call for drastic measures.

FREDDIE. How long have you been in my hotel room?

LIZ. I need to talk to you.

FREDDIE. Who let you in here? What the fuck is wrong with you?

LIZ. It's not important.

FREDDIE. Are you a stalker or an agent?

LIZ. Tomato, Tomahto. I needed to speak with you in private.

FREDDIE. Then hit me up like a normal person.

LIZ. You're not answering my calls, Freddie. I thought we had a trust between us.

FREDDIE. Trust my ass, everywhere I look someone's bashing me.

LIZ. That's not my fault.

FREDDIE. What the fuck are you doing about it?

LIZ. We need to work together on this.

FREDDIE. This fucking sucks and I'm fuckin' ragin', Liz.

LIZ. At me? What did I do to piss you off?

FREDDIE. Everyone's fucking laughing at me.

LIZ. You made a mistake.

FREDDIE. Those reporters were trying to start shit with me.

LIZ. You're supposed to say, "no comment."

FREDDIE. I had never been in a situation like that, Liz. They're calling me a thug. I just lost my fucking temper, it was an honest mistake.

LIZ. It's a business. Press needs to make money too. They make this a bigger deal than it really is to pay their mortgage.

FREDDIE. I'm not that guy. Everywhere I look I see my face but I don't recognize myself.

LIZ. You've gotta trust me.

FREDDIE. All of a sudden everyone's turning to me for money. I've got long lost cousins calling me "Primo spot me a couple thousand." Or "What's good fam, can you pay my rent this month?" Everyone wants a piece. Why should I trust you?

LIZ. What year were you born?

FREDDIE. 1995.

LIZ. Fuck. That was a terrible year. I lost Karl Malone to CAA and got my car stolen.

FREDDIE. Way to cheer me up Liz.

LIZ. Back in 1995 life was very different. Biggie was still alive. We barely had cell phones, they weighed ten pounds and never had good reception. The internet was new and nobody trusted it. Fax machines and beepers were in. I wore shoulder pads for Christ's sake.

FREDDIE. What's your point?

LIZ. When you're in 1995 you think that life will always be that way. You think that's the end all be all, but then you wake up to your iPhone ringtone and your flat-screen TV and it's 2015. Everything is different. 1995 is a distant past. You'll probably laugh about this when you're my age from your spaceship or whatever the fuck you will drive in the future.

FREDDIE. You really wore shoulder pads?

LIZ. I rocked those motherfuckers like I invented them.

(**FREDDIE** *grabs a photograph from his desk.*)

(*He hands the picture to* **LIZ**.)

LIZ. Nice house.

FREDDIE. I bought it for my Mom, just like I said I would.

LIZ. Funny, I also bought my Dad a house when I got my first big check.

FREDDIE. Where's your Dad's house?

LIZ. Long Island. He didn't believe it was his. He refused to go inside until I showed him the contract.

FREDDIE. Does he still live there?

LIZ. He's dead.

FREDDIE. Word? What happened to him?

LIZ. You don't want to know.

FREDDIE. I do.

LIZ. He threw in the towel, let's leave it at that. I had just been promoted to an agent, it was my first week. I threw myself into my work, I vowed to never give up, no matter how hard life gets. The day my father died was the day that I was born. Life tests us Freddie, this is your test.

FREDDIE. What if I fail?

LIZ. Don't make it an option. Failure is not an option.

FREDDIE. My mom's really proud of me. This house I bought comes with a pool, a two-car garage, even hired my mom a maid. Her whole life she's been breaking her back to clean up other people's messes. Now she's got someone to do that for her, so she can chill… I don't want to lose this. Please help me. Please.

LIZ. First things first. You need to be on your best behavior. Monastic shit. Give me your phone.

FREDDIE. What?

> (**LIZ** *gets up and searches the room. She finds the phone and grabs it before he can.*)

FREDDIE. That's my personal business, don't look at that.

> (**LIZ** *goes through his texts.*)

LIZ. Okay, any woman who texts you a coochie shot is not someone you need to be talking to right now.

FREDDIE. I'm a man. I've got needs.

LIZ. It's called porn, Freddie. You'll live.

FREDDIE. I need physical contact, Liz. I need the release.

LIZ. Release into your own hand, buddy. I don't want to Google you tomorrow and find a dick pic on TMZ. You feel me?

FREDDIE. Fuck…this is gonna be tough.

LIZ. Your image needs a makeover.

FREDDIE. Maybe I can be a bad boy, like Bill Lambier.

LIZ. Honey, if Bill Lambier looked like us, they would have kicked his ass out onto the streets.

FREDDIE. …did I fuck it up, Liz? Honestly.

>*(A beat. **FREDDIE**'s dreams are slipping away from him.)*

LIZ. Lucky for you, I'm a PR God. I represented Dennis Rodman during the "Bad As I Wanna Be" era. If I can keep him afloat through his dress-wearing, head-butting, Madonna-fucking days, I can certainly manage this.

FREDDIE. Dennis Rodman won five NBA championships, was a two-time Allstar, two-time defensive player of the year, AND was a seven-time NBA rebounding champ.

LIZ. Yes, I'm aware.

FREDDIE. I just started my career. I've barely played enough minutes to get good stats.

>*(**LIZ** paces. This is going to be a tough one. She picks up the phone.)*

LIZ. Hi, can I get a whiskey neat and a…

>*(**LIZ** motions to **FREDDIE**.)*

FREDDIE. Can I have some milk, please?

>*(A beat. **LIZ** looks at **FREDDIE** for a moment. She sees a child inside a man's body.)*

FREDDIE. What?

LIZ. Nothing.

*(**LIZ** continues ordering on the phone.)*

LIZ. So one whiskey neat and a milk.

FREDDIE. With chocolate.

LIZ. Make that a chocolate milk.

*(**LIZ** hangs up the phone.)*

FREDDIE. It helps me calm my nerves.

LIZ. You can trust me, buddy. My clients mean everything to me, my clients are my legacy.

FREDDIE. I don't want to be remembered this way.

LIZ. You won't. I'm gonna get you a really classy interview with Barbara Flowers. A prime time special report.

FREDDIE. More interviews? I don't know Liz.

LIZ. This one will be under my control.

FREDDIE. You can't control those reporters, they're crazy.

LIZ. Barbara and I go way back. She's Mr. Candy's cousin.

FREDDIE. You trust her?

LIZ. The interview will be scripted. Barbara will stick to the script. I'll get Coach Jones on board. It will be great.

FREDDIE. What am I gonna say?

LIZ. We will go over it in detail over the next couple of days. You'll be completely prepared.

FREDDIE. You really think this is gonna work?

LIZ. I'll get you out of this mess, I promise. I'll protect you.

FREDDIE. Thanks Liz. You know, they were wrong about you.

LIZ. I don't really care what people think of me.

FREDDIE. Good because everyone I know is intimidated by you.

LIZ. And you?

FREDDIE. Nah, I feel like I know you deep down inside. You're a nice lady when no one is looking.

(Lights out.)

Wine and Dine

(An elegant restaurant. **COACH JONES** *sits at a table; he's wearing a suit and tie.)*

*(***LIZ*** *enters, she's wearing a sexy dress.)*

LIZ. Waiting long?

COACH JONES. Ten minutes.

*(***LIZ*** *sits.)*

LIZ. You ordered me a martini?

COACH JONES. Did you want something else?

LIZ. It's fine.

COACH JONES. Good. Good.

(A beat. **LIZ** *looks over her menu.)*

LIZ. What are you getting?

COACH JONES. You're paying?

LIZ. The company is.

COACH JONES. Lobster.

LIZ. Still cheap, I see.

COACH JONES. And I'm ordering a bottle of Cristal for the table.

LIZ. Ya, fine whatever. Get two. So…what do you want?

COACH JONES. Can't we have a friendly dinner?

LIZ. I'm not friendly, you know that.

COACH JONES. But you're in the people business.

LIZ. I fucking hate people. They never know what they want. They just want to bother you with their indecision. People lie to you. People shit on you. People love you when you have something they want. In my spare time I prefer solitude. I look forward to it.

COACH JONES. Solitude?

LIZ. I had a cat, Mr. Kitty, but I gave it away. I need to be completely alone for a certain number of hours of the day, or else I will lose my shit. Where's the waiter? I'm starving.

*(**LIZ** looks for the waiter.)*

COACH JONES. I'm extending my friendship here.

LIZ. I stopped believing in friendship when I got rich.

COACH JONES. That's a sad thought.

LIZ. Eat or get eaten. It's my world. I'm not complaining.

COACH JONES. Fine, don't be my friend. I don't care.

LIZ. Typical.

COACH JONES. What?

LIZ. You think you're the center of the fucking universe. Well, not mine, maybe someone else's but not mine.

COACH JONES. It's like I'm eating dinner with a block of ice.

LIZ. Poor baby.

COACH JONES. Fuck you, Liz.

LIZ. For that I'm making you pay for the drinks.

COACH JONES. Let's just talk about Luna. What's the plan?

LIZ. Barbara Flowers. We do a special about where he's from. Show clips of the Red Hook projects and Flowers will ask Luna questions about his past. He apologizes, a couple tears would be nice, and then BAM, we're back in business.

COACH JONES. It's as easy as that.

LIZ. Yup.

COACH JONES. I hate to say it, but…

LIZ. Then don't say it.

COACH JONES. I told you so.

LIZ. That's all you wanted, isn't it. You have nothing better to do than make me feel small.

COACH JONES. I love being right, Liz. You know that.

LIZ. There's a lot on the line with this kid. Candy will leave me his company IF Luna makes it big.

COACH JONES. What are you doing with your life?

LIZ. Excuse me? You want to pay for your fucking lobster, son?

COACH JONES. Candy tells you to jump, you jump. Candy tells you to play puppet master with this poor innocent kid and you have your hand up his ass. Making him say whatever. This kid isn't ready.

LIZ. What if you're wrong?

COACH JONES. You're not in the trenches every day. You're not on the court, in the locker room. I know Luna. He's got a lot of growing up to do.

LIZ. You've been wrong before.

COACH JONES. You want your name on some office door and in the process you're going to destroy someone's life.

LIZ. What the fuck do you know?

COACH JONES. I know you. Last month you went on a drunken rant about leaving Mr. Candy high and dry but you woke up hungover and took it all back. Said you didn't mean it.

LIZ. You're a disgruntled little coach. You have absolutely no power within that organization. You're aching to shit on someone and I'm the closest person around. You're a pathetic man.

(A beat.)

(LIZ drinks her martini. COACH JONES finishes his cocktail. Liquid courage.)

COACH JONES. I want you to sit on my face, so I can make you come so hard that your screams could shatter a glass window.

(A beat. Sexual tension.)

LIZ. I thought we said that last time would be the LAST.

COACH JONES. You've got me chocolate pussy whipped. Marry me?

LIZ. You're just lonely.

COACH JONES. I'm not. I have options.

LIZ. You're just plain stupid then.

COACH JONES. I can't stop thinking about the last time. It was a half marathon of fucking, my back still hurts but I can't stop smiling. I'm wondering if we can give it another go.

LIZ. I'm not promising anything.

COACH JONES. You can't tell me that you didn't have a great time. You were making animal sounds.

LIZ. I'm not confirming or denying it. We're talking about the present here.

COACH JONES. We could make a good team off the court.

LIZ. I've been down this road several times with other men, Jones. It never works out.

COACH JONES. I'm not like other men.

LIZ. Because you're a bottom?

COACH JONES. Because I know you. Like REALLY know you. Professionally and personally. For years.

LIZ. It never works out, so I stopped trying. I'm married to my clients.

COACH JONES. That's very disappointing.

LIZ. Last year I made the Forbes' "50 Most Powerful Women in the Country" list. That's enough for me.

COACH JONES. You can have both.

LIZ. No one can have both.

COACH JONES. I'm successful and I'm very understanding.

LIZ. You are now. But the seventh time in a row that I have to fly out on your birthday for a client, the fifteenth time I cancel our anniversary dinner, the understanding will melt away. I'm operating at a high level, Bill. It's not fair to anyone.

COACH JONES. You've never even been married.

LIZ. Yesterday was my work anniversary, twenty-three years at The Candy Agency so I decided to celebrate. I worked until 7 p.m., which is early for me. Then I went home and had three tins of gold Imperial Caviar with crackers and a bottle of Johnnie Walker Blue for dinner. I was naked in my penthouse with floor to ceiling windows. I turned off my phone and watched the sun creep behind Jersey. The orange and pink streaks of heaven that peek out from behind the majestic Manhattan skyline. And it hit me, I just plain forgot to have children and a husband. I didn't mind it at all.

COACH JONES. I don't want you to be alone. I care about you.

LIZ. I want to be alone. I want to run shit, babe. Power's not something you share.

> *(A beat. This is not the response that* COACH *was hoping for.)*

COACH JONES. You're a phenomenal woman. I just wanted to take care of you, is all. I think I can do that.

LIZ. That's my kryptonite, Coach.

COACH JONES. I see.

> *(A beat.* COACH JONES *sinks his head into his menu. He's sulking, this wasn't the way this dinner was supposed to go.)*

> *(*LIZ *sips on her martini and watches him.)*

LIZ. Ready to order?

COACH JONES. I'm not so hungry anymore. Maybe just drinks and dessert.

LIZ. Oh okay.

COACH JONES. …

LIZ. Want to come over tonight? For old time's sake? I have more caviar in the fridge. No strings attached, I'll just ride you like a rodeo. Sound fun?

COACH JONES. Maybe we should just stick to business.

LIZ. Sure. Fine.

> *(*COACH JONES *and* LIZ *stare into their menus.)*

> *(Lights out.)*

Barbara Flowers Special Report

(A studio set.)

(BARBARA FLOWERS, FREDDIE, COACH JONES,
and **LIZ** *sit in front of a film crew.)*

(BARBARA *speaks out to the audience.)*

BARBARA FLOWERS. Good evening, I'm Barbara Flowers
and tonight we have a special report on NBA superstar
rookie Freddie Luna. Luna's antics are a hot topic
of discussion across the country. Last week he lost
his temper during a post-game press conference and
attacked his coach. Freddie's past doesn't help his
image, he's from the rough neighborhood of Red
Hook, Brooklyn and at nineteen has already spent a
lengthy amount of time in a Juvenile Detention Center.
Is Freddie actually the thug he's recently been labeled
by the media or is he a glimmer of hope for the
struggling Knicks franchise? This evening, we sit down
with Freddie, his coach, Bill Jones, and his agent Liz
Rico to find out who the real Freddie Luna is.

(Cue the theme song.)

Welcome, everyone.

FREDDIE. Thank you for having me Barbara, I'm a huge
fan.

BARBARA FLOWERS. Freddie, if there was anything you
could say to your fans right now, anything at all, what
would it be?

FREDDIE. I'd like to apologize for my behavior. There are
no excuses for my actions. I'm sorry to the fans and to
the Knicks organization.

COACH JONES. Barbara, Freddie's a great kid. He's
extremely talented with lots of potential, but potential
must be cultivated. There are lots of organizations out
there that want talent without helping shape it. The
New York Knicks are not one of them.

BARBARA FLOWERS. So Freddie, what consequences will you face because of your actions?

FREDDIE. I've been fined by the league and I've been benched for three games. I just want to play basketball. It's been my dream since I was a little boy. I've learned from my mistakes and just want to move forward.

BARBARA FLOWERS. Liz, you signed Freddie from a Red Hook High School basketball team and got him a multi million dollar contract with the New York Knicks. Why Freddie?

LIZ. That's a great question Barbara and I love your suit.

BARBARA FLOWERS. Oh, thank you.

LIZ. Freddie Luna's story is tragic; his father was murdered when Freddie was four. His mother was deported to Venezuela. Freddie has been in and out of foster care. He spent his teens sharing a two-bedroom apartment in the projects with ten other people. He's lost many friends to gang violence and drugs. But when I met this young man, his fortitude and ambition really struck me. I thought, this kid's really going to make it.

BARBARA FLOWERS. Were you aware of Freddie's criminal record?

LIZ. I was Barbara. But everyone deserves a second chance, especially people like Freddie who are born into difficult circumstances. In today's world these young men of color don't even get a first chance. Trayvon Martin, Michael Brown, and Tamir Rice deserved the opportunity to make mistakes, they deserved a fair shot at life. If Freddie was of another race you wouldn't think twice about this.

BARBARA FLOWERS. So it's racism?

COACH JONES. I think that Liz is referring to the negative press that's been coming out recently. Freddie's been called several names, including a "thug," a "criminal," etcetera. What happened between Freddie and I didn't warrant these allegations. The media took what happened and ran with it.

BARBARA FLOWERS. How does this make you feel, Freddie?

FREDDIE. I'm not gonna lie. I'm upset about it.

> *(A beat.)*
>
> *(**LIZ RICO** is overjoyed by **FREDDIE**'s emotional honesty but tries her best to hide it.)*

LIZ. Do you need a tissue, Freddie?

> *(**COACH JONES** gives **LIZ** a nudge to stop taking pleasure in this boy's pain.)*

COACH JONES. You okay kid?

FREDDIE. I just want a chance to prove to everyone what I can do. It's a dream come true to put on that NBA jersey. A couple of months ago, I had posters hanging in my locker of my teammates and now they are my friends. It's crazy. I don't want it to end because of my temper. I'm truly sorry.

BARBARA FLOWERS. Freddie, reports state that the two boys whom you allegedly assaulted have been coming to your Knicks games in protest. They've rallied outside of Madison Square Garden pleading that you be taken off the team because of your alleged crime. Are you aware of this?

LIZ. He doesn't have to speak about this. You don't have to answer that Freddie.

FREDDIE. It's okay. I haven't seen them but I've heard about them.

BARBARA FLOWERS. You claim you're innocent but served six months in a Youth Detention Center for brutally assaulting Ronald Smith and Peter Jordan. One of whom you left in a wheelchair for life.

FREDDIE. I'm innocent. I did someone else's time.

BARBARA FLOWERS. You're covering for someone else? Are you familiar with the legal terms "accessory" or "accomplice"? Depending upon the degree of your participation in the assault, you would still be at fault.

FREDDIE. Barbara, where I come from, nobody likes a snitch. I'm better off serving my time and keeping my mouth shut.

BARBARA FLOWERS. So the person who hurt those boys, left one without an eye and the other paralyzed for life, that person is still out there roaming the streets?

FREDDIE. Yes.

BARBARA FLOWERS. And you know the identity of this person but won't tell authorities?

LIZ. He's not going to go any further with this, Barbara.

BARBARA FLOWERS. Let him respond, Liz. It's just a question.

COACH JONES. The league doesn't want him speaking on this subject.

FREDDIE. Hold up. Barbara, I didn't hurt those guys. I'm innocent. I want everyone watching to know that.

BARBARA FLOWERS. Freddie, you are an accessory or possible accomplice to assault and battery. According to the law, you are by no means innocent.

FREDDIE. You can't say that. What the fuck.

COACH JONES. *(to* **FREDDIE***)* Calm down.

BARBARA FLOWERS. I have a law degree and this is my show, I can say anything I damn well please.

FREDDIE. Liz? She's not sticking to the script.

LIZ. All right, I'm pulling him.

BARBARA FLOWERS. Liz, you're being touchy. Come on.

LIZ. Freddie take off your mic.

COACH JONES. *(to* **LIZ***)* Don't let them use this footage.

BARBARA FLOWERS. Wait, Freddie, let's discuss your mother. She was deported in 2009, what are your thoughts on immigration law in this country?

LIZ. This interview is over. Mics off, cameras off, let's go.

> *(***FREDDIE*** and* **COACH JONES** *stand and start to remove their mics.)*

BARBARA FLOWERS. Freddie we reached your mother, Susana Flores Luna. She gave us a quote. It's in Spanish /but we've translated…

FREDDIE. You told my mom about this? Are you fucking serious? Liz, what the fuck?

LIZ. This is below the belt Barbara, this is low.

BARBARA FLOWERS. Susana said, "It's my fault. I did the best I could but I wish I had been a better mother. I let my son down."

> (**FREDDIE** *lunges at* **BARBARA**.)

FREDDIE. That's my family, you white devil bitch!

BARBARA FLOWERS. Calm him down!

> (**LIZ** *tries to hold* **FREDDIE** *back, but he's lost his shit.*)

FREDDIE. My family's all I got! Don't fuck with them!

LIZ. No/ Stop the cameras!

BARBARA FLOWERS. Security!/ Security!

COACH JONES. Freddie/ stop!

> (**BARBARA** *hides behind* **COACH JONES** *who shields her from* **FREDDIE**'s *rage.*)

FREDDIE. Leave my family alone! You hear me?!?

> (*Lights out.*)

Shitty Shit

*(**LIZ**'s office. **GABBY** and **LIZ** are on their respective phone calls.)*

LIZ. I don't care about her ratings, she screwed me… that wasn't the agreement. If Barbara presses charges on Freddie then I'll press charges on her…breach of contract… It was a verbal agreement between me and that lying whore… Don't tell her I said that… I don't give a shit about her ratings. She can shove them up her skinny little ass…

*(**GABBY** waves at **LIZ**.)*

GABBY. I've got Kevin Love on the phone.

LIZ. *(whispers to **GABBY**)* I'll call him back.

GABBY. He's called five times within forty-eight hours. I think he really needs to talk.

LIZ. I'll call him back.

GABBY.	**LIZ**.
(into the phone) Kevin, she's not available… I'm so sorry. I know. I know.	*(into the phone)* You there? I want action not your apologies. Just do it.

*(**LIZ** hangs up the phone.)*

GABBY. Do you want lunch? I haven't seen you eat in forty-eight hours.

LIZ. Get me a tuna melt and an attorney.

GABBY. Who exactly?

LIZ. Some hotshot civil rights attorney. I don't care how young or old they are. We need the best.

GABBY. Okay.

LIZ. Make sure Freddie makes it to practice today.

GABBY. You want me to call him a car?

LIZ. Yes, call him my car. Make Luis get out of the car and drag him by the ear to practice.

GABBY. Got it.

LIZ. Has Barbara called back?

GABBY. Nope.

LIZ. What an asshole. Call her again.

GABBY. I don't think I should.

LIZ. I don't care what you think.

GABBY. Between Freddie's calls and your calls, I think Barbara's pretty fed up.

LIZ. Does it look like I give a fuck? Does it?

GABBY. You were subpoenaed this morning. She is putting a restraining order on you and Freddie.

LIZ. Cunty. Cunt face. Send it to Candy's attorney. Get him on the line, please.

GABBY. There are some other people looking for you.

LIZ. Who?

GABBY. You've got a ton of messages, Liz.

LIZ. Okay, shoot.

GABBY. Kevin Love. He sounds pissed.

LIZ. He'll survive.

GABBY. Carmelo called yesterday and you never returned his call. James Harden called about the new Taco Bell commercials. And Anthony Davis has texted you seven times asking about his Gatorade deal.

LIZ. Okay. Fine. Get Candy's attorney on the line.

GABBY. What should I say to the others?

LIZ. They can wait. All of them. Tell them to wait.

GABBY. Every time they call, they get bitchier and bitchier.

LIZ. Get tougher skin, Gabby.

GABBY. Love said that CAA has been calling him non-stop.

LIZ. Oh please. Love isn't leaving.

GABBY. How do you know?

LIZ. He loves me. No pun intended.

GABBY. You won't call him back.

LIZ. I will, later. I'll get to it. You have to prioritize.

GABBY. Kevin's a huge client. He's not a priority all of a sudden?

LIZ. Are you married to him or something?

GABBY. No, I'm just asking about your strategy. Trying to learn and observe. Isn't every client relationship supposed to be a priority?

LIZ. I don't like your tone.

GABBY. I have no tone, I'm just asking you a question.

LIZ. Keep the attitude at a minimum and get me a stiff drink.

GABBY. Do you want me to dial Kevin or Carmelo or Anthony Davis?

LIZ. Did I ask for that?

GABBY. No, but…

LIZ. Do what I ask of you. It's not that hard of a job.

> (**GABBY** *nods. She goes to the mini bar and pours* **LIZ** *a drink.*)

> (*A beeping alert is heard from* **GABBY**'s *computer.*)

LIZ. What is that?

GABBY. Five oh, five oh.

> (**LIZ** *panics.*)

LIZ. SHIT. ETA?

GABBY. Less than one min/ute.

> (**MR. CANDY** *enters.*)

MR. CANDY. Liz? A word?

LIZ. Yes, Mr. Candy.

MR. CANDY. May I sit.

LIZ. Of course. Gabby? Get him a drink?

MR. CANDY. No, thanks.

LIZ. How can I help you?

MR. CANDY. How can I help YOU?

LIZ. Everything's great. Just peachy.

MR. CANDY. Have you lost your mind? This Luna kid's a sinking ship.

LIZ. Why did you beg me to sign him?

MR. CANDY. Liz, I just came from a board conference call about you and how much you fucked this up. Phil Stern is twerking in the lunch room, all hell's breakin' loose my dear.

LIZ. The board is "intimidated" by me. They don't want me running the company. You said it yourself.

MR. CANDY. We want you to drop Luna.

LIZ. What?

MR. CANDY. The board's down my throat. Barbara Flowers is up my ass. Everyone wants blood.

LIZ. I've been through worse situations with clients. I can get him out of this.

MR. CANDY. You're in over your head.

LIZ. I'm not.

MR. CANDY. I've gotten calls from Kevin Love, Carmelo Anthony and James Harden. They're complaining about your lack of attentiveness lately.

LIZ. I see.

> (**LIZ** *smells a rat. She makes eye contact with* **GABBY**. **GABBY** *avoids her gaze.*)

MR. CANDY. I figure that you drop Luna and you get back to normal.

LIZ. Kick him when he's down.

MR. CANDY. You're not yourself.

LIZ. In what sense?

MR. CANDY. Distracted by the kid. He's one name on an elite client list that you've built over several years.

LIZ. He's in trouble. I'm trying to get him out of it.

MR. CANDY. It's not worth it.

LIZ. I see something in him.

MR. CANDY. I miss the old Liz Rico. Get her back here.

LIZ. I'm still Liz.

MR. CANDY. We have history. A long and rich past full of good memories. I hate to tarnish two decades of success over one lousy kid out of Red Hook.

LIZ. …

MR. CANDY. Your hesitance is unnerving.

LIZ. I'm just not sure about this.

MR. CANDY. This is a no-brainer, Liz. Come on. You're the best in the business, this is an easy choice.

LIZ. Normally this would be a no-brainer but I feel responsible for this kid.

MR. CANDY. You need to think of yourself. Of the agency. Not of Luna, he's on his own.

LIZ. Yes. Right.

MR. CANDY. Just call him up and apologize profusely. Tell him to get a good therapist and another agent.

LIZ. Okay.

MR. CANDY. Gabby? Can you get Luna on the phone please?

GABBY. Yes, Mr. Candy.

MR. CANDY. Let's get this over with.

(A beat. **GABBY** *dials.)*

LIZ. …Wait.

MR. CANDY. Wait?

LIZ. I…

MR. CANDY. What's the big deal? It's just one kid.

LIZ. He's in trouble.

MR. CANDY. What do you care?

LIZ. I… I don't know.

MR. CANDY. Liz, you look like hell. You're tired because you've been putting in the effort. I appreciate it, don't get me wrong. But you're wasting your time at this point.

LIZ. What if you're wrong?

MR. CANDY. Guys like Luna are a dime a dozen. Freddie baffles me. He's got loads of talent and a great agent. Why does he want to fuck it up for himself?

LIZ. He's not doing it on purpose. He just doesn't know any better.

MR. CANDY. And what are you supposed to do about that? Play Mommy?

LIZ. No. I've never wanted kids.

MR. CANDY. Then drop Luna. It's a five minute phone call. Do it and get it done.

LIZ. Let me do it on my own terms. In my own time.

MR. CANDY. No.

LIZ. Why are you pushing?

MR. CANDY. Pull it together. I've offered to leave my entire company to you, don't make me question my decision.

     (A beat.)

LIZ. *(firm)* I'll do it on my own terms. In my own time.

MR. CANDY. It better get done. Today. I'm not fucking around Elizabeth.

     *(**MR. CANDY** exits. **LIZ** sits back in her chair. What to do?)*

GABBY. Do you want me to get Luna on the phone?

LIZ. …

GABBY. Liz?

LIZ. …

GABBY. You should eat something. Then we can call Luna. Okay? Let me get you that tuna melt, stat.

LIZ. Go home Gabby.

GABBY. What? Why?

LIZ. Take the rest of the day off.

GABBY. Am I in trouble?

LIZ. No.

GABBY. Good because I haven't done anything wrong.

LIZ. Are you talking to Candy behind my back?

GABBY. No.

LIZ. Whose side do you think you're on?

GABBY. Liz, I'm grateful for everything you've taught me but it's time I branch out on my own.

LIZ. You think you're ready for that?

GABBY. Yes. Absolutely.

LIZ. Do what you want. If Candy's offering you a promotion for ratting me out, you should take it but be prepared for the consequences.

GABBY. Candy did offer me a job.

LIZ. What did you give him in return?

GABBY. What are you offering me? I need the job. I need the money.

LIZ. Integrity. You stick with the people who helped you when you were nothing.

GABBY. Integrity?

LIZ. Yes.

GABBY. I've watched you be deceitful and dirty for the past five years. Freddie Luna? You've ruined his life so that you could get ahead. Your sense of "integrity" is fucked up.

> (**GABBY** *exits in a blind rage.*)

LIZ. *(yells after her)* Go cry to Mr. Candy. He'll dry your tears.

> *(A beat.)*

> (**LIZ** *sits at her desk quietly. Perhaps some of what* **GABBY** *said resonated with her.*)

> (**LIZ** *picks up her desk phone and dials a number.*)

> *(Split stage,* **FREDDIE LUNA***'s wearing workout clothes. He's walking home post practice. His phone rings, he answers.*)

LIZ. Freddie. It's Liz.

FREDDIE. What's up Liz? I'm walking into practice.

LIZ. Listen, kid. I'm gonna make this quick and painless.

FREDDIE. What's going on?

LIZ. I can't be your agent anymore.

FREDDIE. Oh.

LIZ. Don't worry about the Barbara Flowers thing. The agency will cover your legal expenses. You can call me anytime to check in, I just can't advise you professionally anymore.

FREDDIE. Why? Are you mad at me?

LIZ. No, not at all Freddie. This is strictly about business.

FREDDIE. Uh...

LIZ. Hello? Are you there? Do you understand what I'm saying?

FREDDIE. I understand, yes.

LIZ. Okay, good.

FREDDIE. I don't know what I'm supposed to say.

LIZ. You'll be fine. You keep playing and get your temper under control. Okay? You'll be good.

FREDDIE. So this is about the Barbara Flowers interview?

LIZ. The company's just going in a different direction right now. The market dictates where we will go and there's been a shift. It happens.

FREDDIE. Okay...

LIZ. Take care, okay Freddie?

FREDDIE. Ya whatever.

> (**FREDDIE** *hangs up on* **LIZ**. **LIZ** *gets up and pours herself a drink. She tries to take a sip but can't. She throws the glass of whiskey across the room. The glass shatters.*)
>
> (*Lights out.*)

Get It Gurl

> *(MR. CANDY stands at a podium in a boardroom with a glass of champagne. He speaks directly to the audience as if they are the board members. MR. CANDY taps the champagne glass with a spoon to get everyone's attention.)*

MR. CANDY. Good afternoon, everyone. I'll make this quick since we all have business to attend to. With a heavy heart, I announce my retirement from The Candy Agency. I assure you that I'll be leaving you all in good hands. The best. Ladies and Gentleman, let me introduce you to your fearless new leader: Elizabeth Rico, CEO of The Candy Agency.

> *(We hear clapping as LIZ enters, she gives MR. CANDY a hug.)*

LIZ. Thank you, Mr. Candy.

MR. CANDY. You're very welcome.

LIZ. I've known Mr. Candy for a long, long time, now.

MR. CANDY. Don't give away my age, dear.

LIZ. I know what he looked like before the grays, before he was married. It has been a pleasure, sir. I feel like we've grown up together.

MR. CANDY. The pleasure's been mine. I'll let you address your team.

> *(MR. CANDY takes a step back and lets LIZ take center stage.)*

LIZ. *(to the group)* I'm honored that Mr. Candy has allowed me the opportunity to run this magnificent sports agency. I started working for Mr. Candy when I was twenty-one years old. A recent Yale graduate, I had the ambition and drive to make something of myself. Mr. Candy invested in me when I was a diamond in the rough, a girl from the projects with a dream, and he taught me how to identify that tenacity and potential in my clients. Here at The Candy Agency, we pride ourselves on our client relationships. We want to grow with our clients. We want to find those diamonds in the rough and nurture them into success. We want to invest in young athletes, that's what the Candy Agency /stands for…

> *(**GABBY** rushes in and interrupts **LIZ** mid-speech.*
> *(**GABBY** whispers something into **LIZ**'s ear. **LIZ***
> *receives shocking news and tries her best to hide it.)*

You'll have to excuse me. A family emergency has just… I have to excuse myself. I'm very sorry.

> *(**LIZ** exits abruptly. **GABBY** quickly follows.)*

> *(Lights out.)*

Guilt

(A hospital waiting room. **COACH JONES** *is on his cell phone.)*

COACH JONES. No comment and stop calling, have some fucking decency.

*(***COACH JONES*** *hangs up as* **LIZ** *enters in a rush.)*

LIZ. Can I see him? Where is he?

COACH JONES. The league suspended him for a year and the Knicks terminated his contract.
He took it pretty hard.

LIZ. I heard.

COACH JONES. I guess his well-being isn't your concern anymore because he isn't a client.

LIZ. It was a business decision.

COACH JONES. Save the bullshit for the office, Liz.

LIZ. I think we can do without the insults, all right Bill?

COACH JONES. I was on my way to kick him out of the Knicks' housing and I saw him there on the pavement. He fucking jumped.

LIZ. When can I see him?

COACH JONES. He's in surgery now but he was asking for you before they put him under.

LIZ. What did he say?

COACH JONES. Mostly gibberish. He should be dead.

LIZ. I can't fucking believe this. I just can't.

COACH JONES. I couldn't get a hold of his mother.

LIZ. I had Gabby call before I left the office. She already knew about it from the news. There's a media shitstorm outside.

COACH JONES. And he left a note for you.

LIZ. For me?

COACH JONES. It's addressed to you. I thought you might want to read it.

(COACH JONES hands LIZ the suicide note. She reads it to herself, then reads out loud.)

LIZ. "Liz, I'm your legacy" …motherfucker… He's such an asshole. I can't even…

COACH JONES. Freddie's not in the right state of mind.

LIZ. I can see the headlines now, "CEO leads ex-client to suicide." Twenty-three motherfucking years mean nothing because of this. Funny how that works out.

COACH JONES. This will blow over, this is about Freddie not you.

LIZ. This will ruin me.

COACH JONES. Liz, I know we've had our ups and downs but trust me, Freddie's decision isn't a reflection of you, get over yourself.

LIZ. Oh fuck you, who are you? Mr. Perfect?

COACH JONES. Look, we're both human and this is a complicated business. You always say "You can't mix the personal with the business."

LIZ. I broke my own rule.

(The cap that LIZ uses to keep her emotions hidden has burst off. LIZ tries to hide her tears from COACH JONES.)

(He tries to embrace her. She pushes him away.)

LIZ. Bill. I think I just need a minute.

COACH JONES. I'm not leaving.

LIZ. Just a fucking minute. I just don't understand it, Bill. I could have given up a million times but I never did. I don't understand.

COACH JONES. Freddie's not built like you are. You're invincible.

LIZ. I'm not.

COACH JONES. You're the strongest person I know.

LIZ. I've been scared all this time. Terrified.

COACH JONES. You don't act like it.

LIZ. I've been trying to cram myself into this box for years…but that's just not me… It's not me…

(Lights out.)

Equity, Bitch

(A couple weeks later.)

*(**LIZ**'s office, which is now **GABBY**'s office, is redecorated and has **GABBY**'s diplomas hanging from the walls.)*

*(**GABBY** sits behind her desk; she's on the phone, mid-conversation.)*

GABBY. Marc. Marc? Marc. MARC. His stats say it all. He's up in rebounds and steals. He's a role player. Marc. I don't care if you don't like his wife, just pay him what he's worth! I'm going to give you twenty-four hours to counter Miami's offer.

*(**LIZ** enters.)*

*(**GABBY** waves her over to have a seat.)*

Marc, if not we are walking. Marc? Marc. Do you… Do you hear… Got it? He's excited about Miami but he'd rather play for you… Okay good. Bye.

*(**GABBY** hangs up the phone.)*

Coño, hijo de la gran…

LIZ. Marc Cuban?

GABBY. How the fuck did you ever get a word in with that guy?

LIZ. Just tell him how great he is, he loves that. All the owners have different ways of running their teams. What are you gonna do?

GABBY. Strangle him.

LIZ. You'll be okay, just remember to be firm. Stand your ground.

GABBY. I know, Liz. I know. So? What's going on?

LIZ. This is a little odd, isn't it?

GABBY. "It's good to be king," Liz.

LIZ. Cute. I'm happy the office went to someone like you. I don't think I said this enough when you worked for me Gabby, but you're as good as gold. Truly.

> (*A beat.* GABBY*'s taken aback by the compliment. She grows skeptical of* LIZ.)

GABBY. That's uncharacteristically nice of you.

LIZ. I mean it.

GABBY. I still don't get it. You had it all and you just walked away. I'm still waiting for you to bust down my door wanting your office back.

LIZ. I had a change of heart. That's why I'm here actually. I'm going to start my own agency.

GABBY. Uh…okay…

LIZ. We're going to be small at first.

GABBY. Well, yah, I mean you have no clients.

LIZ. But I will.

GABBY. Who? They all stayed at The Candy Agency, either with me or Mr. Candy.

LIZ. Honey, I let you have those clients. That was a gift.

GABBY. Okay, here we go.

LIZ. I'm not here to argue.

GABBY. Fine. You have a clientless new agency. Congrats. I wish you the best.

LIZ. You wish me the best. Don't play dumb with me, you know what comes next.

GABBY. What is it?

LIZ. You're not going to make this easy for me, are you.

GABBY. Nope, not one bit.

> (LIZ *laughs.*)

If you're doing what I think you're doing, I would appreciate a formal offer. I mean, if that's why you are here.

LIZ. Gabby, I'm here because I want you to come work for my company. It's a big decision, I know that. But take some time to think /about it.

GABBY. I want health insurance.

LIZ. Done.

GABBY. A signing bonus.

LIZ. Sure.

GABBY. Really?

LIZ. I'm serious.

GABBY. I want…equity.

LIZ. You'll have it.

GABBY. WHAT? REALLY?

LIZ. Yes.

GABBY. Bullshit, you hate sharing. You're going to give me shares of your brand new company just because I asked you for them?

LIZ. I'll do whatever it takes.

GABBY. I'm very happy here, Liz. I have a great relationship with Mr. Candy. I've been promoted, given a hefty raise and I'm on track to make partner.

LIZ. You'd have to give those things up, but I will do everything in my power to ensure that we are successful.

GABBY. You can't "ensure" anything in this business.

LIZ. It's called, faith. I hired you five years ago when you were twenty pounds heavier and your speaking voice was as loud as a whisper. I miss that girl, I had faith in her.

GABBY. We are at very different places in our lives. It's a big risk for me.

LIZ. Whatever you're feeling deep down inside, that's what you should do. I can't tell you what that is.

*(A beat. **GABBY** thinks about it.)*

GABBY. I'm going to stay here, Liz. I'm very sorry.

(A beat.)

*(**LIZ** takes this in; she's disappointed but she hides it.)*

LIZ. Don't you dare be sorry. You've made a decision and as a woman I respect that.

GABBY. Liz, I owe a lot to you, really.

LIZ. No Gabby. You're family to me, I'm just… I'm not good at letting people know.

*(**LIZ** exits.)*

*(A beat. **GABBY** exhales and looks around the office she's worked so hard to get.)*

(Lights out.)

Crossroad

(A hospital room. The bed's empty and unmade.
FREDDIE LUNA *sits in a wheelchair and stares out*
the window. Both of his legs have casts on them.)

*(**LIZ** enters, she's surprised to see him out of bed.)*

LIZ. Hey. Feeling/ better?

FREDDIE. What the fuck are you doing here?

LIZ. You asked for me before your first surgery. It took me
a while to get here.

FREDDIE. Fine. You showed up. Good job. Now get the fuck
out.

LIZ. No.

FREDDIE. You're not my friend. You're not my agent. You're
nothing to me.

LIZ. Why would you do this to yourself?

FREDDIE. I'll call security on your ass.

LIZ. You're in the psych ward, babe. They're not gonna
listen to you.

*(**FREDDIE** turns his face away from **LIZ**. He's upset*
with her but also ashamed of himself.)

LIZ. Look, you don't know this yet but life's a long journey
full of peaks and valleys.

FREDDIE. Spare me the speech.

LIZ. Trust me, Freddie, life's about so much more than
basketball.

FREDDIE. Not to you.

LIZ. I've chosen to live a very focused life. You've got
your whole life ahead of you. You can choose to live it
however you want.

FREDDIE. I've got no place to go except back to the
projects. I'd rather kill myself than show my face in
Red Hook again. My mom's really disappointed in me.
You promised me that you wouldn't let this happen.

LIZ. You can be angry with me. But don't be angry with the world, Freddie, trust me. Anger's like putting cement shoes on and trying to run down Canal Street to catch the bus. It won't get you anywhere.

FREDDIE. You talk a lot of game but I think you forgot who you are and where you came from/ Liz.

LIZ. Just stop.

FREDDIE. I heard about Mr. Candy leaving the agency to you if I made it big. You used me.

LIZ. Freddie. This is about you. I'm worried about you.

FREDDIE. You weren't worried about me before when you dropped me over the phone. Over the phone. Like I was nothing to you.

LIZ. I have to live with my mistakes. You have to live with yours. Are you going to be a victim or are you going to be a survivor?

FREDDIE. I tried, Liz. I fucking tried so hard and it led me here.

LIZ. The world's a shitty place. It wasn't built for people like us to be kings.

FREDDIE. No, it wasn't.

LIZ. We have the power to change that. Did you know? We've been blessed with a second shot at life, how are you going to use it? Are you going to sit here and rot away? Or are you going to learn from this and give it another go?

FREDDIE. What do you want from me?

LIZ. I told you, you asked for me so I came.

FREDDIE. Why? You could have blown me off. I know you, you don't do anything unless it benefits you. What's in it for you?

LIZ. Nothing. Absolutely nothing.

> (LIZ *reaches for* FREDDIE*'s hand.* FREDDIE *opens up to her. He lets it all out, his depression, his lack of confidence, his fears, his anger, his loneliness.*)

(**LIZ** *embraces* **FREDDIE**. **FREDDIE**'*s sobs grow louder, deeper; he's realized how shitty life can be but he's made a friend to help him bear it.*)

(Lights out.)

End of Play

CPSIA information can be obtained
at www.ICGtesting.com
Printed in the USA
BVHW041336180921
616799BV00004B/212